Grange Hill For Sale

Could Grange Hill survive? The authorities' statistics about falling rolls of pupils said no, but as Matthew Cartwright and Christopher Stewart found out, figures can be used to prove almost anything.

And it soon becomes clear that the authorities are not Grange Hill's only enemies. Eddie Carver and his mates have old scores to settle, both in school and out. What's more, Eddie is tired of small-time gangland crime and this could be just the chance he is looking for to make his mark in a big way and gain acceptance into the hardened criminal underworld.

To top the lot, there's journalist Jeremy Hart – and whether he is really interested in student rights or just soft on Trisha Yates is anybody's guess.

Also by Robert Leeson in Fontana Lions

GRANGE HILL RULES – OK?
GRANGE HILL GOES WILD
GRANGE HILL HOME AND AWAY
FORTY DAYS OF TUCKER J.
BESS
MAROON BOY
HAROLD AND BELLA, JAMMY AND ME
IT'S MY LIFE
THE THIRD CLASS GENIE

ROBERT LEESON

Grange Hill
For Sale

Based on the BBC television series
GRANGE HILL
by Phil Redmond

FONTANA · LIONS

First published in Fontana Lions 1981
by William Collins Sons & Co. Ltd
8 Grafton Street, London W1X 3LA
Fourth Impression May 1983

Copyright © Robert Leeson and Phil Redmond 1981

Printed in Great Britain by
William Collins Sons & Co. Ltd, Glasgow

TEST YOUR GRANGE HILL KNOWLEDGE

What is the Boot Club and why does Mrs McClusky ban it?
Why is Tucker Jenkins so keen on studying for exams?
Who is Trisha Yates sneaking off with after school?
Why is Precious Matthews running after Benny Green?
And who is running after both of them?
What is the evil Booga Benson back in town for?
Worse still, what is the crafty Eddie Carver up to?
What does Doyle the Boil know which no one else in the
   school knows, and why is he smirking so much?
What has Boris the Computer discovered?
Why are they moving police reinforcements into the area?
What does Pogo Patterson overhear on the loo?
And what does little Belinda get up to when her parents are
   out?

Start at Page 7 and score full marks

Chapter 1

Winter was slowly going and making the usual mess of it. In the park across the street dirty snow streaked the grass and a fine drizzle made the street lights wink.

Belinda Zowkowski heard the car door slam and went to the window to look down. Her parents were off for the evening and she was on her own with a box of candies (correction chocolates) and the TV.

But she didn't switch on the set. They were only showing a series she'd seen two years ago back home in Toronto. She drew the curtains, walked back to the table and pulled out from her school bag a fat little book covered with ancient Snoopy pictures. Tonight was Diary Night and she hadn't written it up for two whole weeks. She crunched a chocolate between her teeth and began.

Dear Diary Person,

Hi! Not much to report. Another day, another dollar (that's 50p at the current rate of exchange) and another country. This time it's England. And another school. It's called Grange Hill.

I'll tell you about the school later. I could write a book about that, and I probably will. I don't know how long I'll be here, in London. Maybe a year, maybe more, till Dad's company ships him, and us, some place else and Mom buys a new easy guide to the next language.

So, they speak English here. I've news. It's another language. A bum doesn't mean a wino. And if you're in lumber it doesn't mean you're in the timber business. When they say sweeping, they mean brooming. A sidewalk's a pavement and a jerk's a good pull. The kids around here ask me stupid questions just to hear me talk. I don't think they're all that mature. But I'll manage.

Who needs friends? No sooner do you get to like someone

7

when – whammo – you're in Wiesbaden or Saudi Arabia and another lot of folk who don't understand you. I'll stick with me.

But Grange Hill, that's something else. There's not another school like it in the galaxy. Dad wanted me to go to a private school but the firm is not about to pay the fees so I go to this state school for free. Free? They should pay you to go there.

Grange Hill has 1000 pupils, every one a nut(job). What's worse, in this country, you swap schools between Grades 5 and 6. Suddenly when you're eleven you're a first year and everybody in the place is bigger than you, knows more than you and lets you know it.

The third years are worst. Making life hard for first years is one of their perks (I'm getting to talk like these folk). Worst of all is one called Gripper. Once he grips you, you are finished. There's only one first year that doesn't reckon to be scared of him and that's Zammo (real name Samuel). No one scares him. One of these days he'll get worked over, for sure. Then there's Jonah (real name Gordon Jones – got it?). He is a sharp dresser, wears so many badges he leans when he walks. There's Fay, she's cool, likes clothes, plays hockey. And Annette, she's just crazy. I quite like her, but who knows if she likes me? Maybe she doesn't even like herself.

What a merry band, ho ho. All we want is to survive this year. After that we get to make life miserable for a new lot of first years.

But wait. A little bird tells me that maybe there won't be any more first years at Grange Hill. We may be the last.

For once I may be around to see something finish.

The word is, Diary, that this school, Grange Hill, is going down the tube.

More later.

Belinda

Chapter 2

Grange Hill was in for a hard time. The message came over loud and clear at the first assembly in the Spring Term. The Headmistress, Mrs McClusky, looked down at the troops as they were drawn up in the hall and spoke in serious tones. It was a solemn occasion and the staff had been persuaded, or ordered, to wear their degree gowns. They even marched in two by two. Miss Lexington looked stunning with her red silk-lined hood. There was handsome Sooty Sutcliffe, Miss Peterson with her white fur-lined cap showing off her dark good looks.

'Hey,' whispered Douglas (Pogo) Patterson out of the corner of his mouth: 'Here's Bullet Baxter, like a gorilla in drag.'

'Sh!' said Claire Scott. 'If Bridget spots your lips moving they'll bounce you out.'

As the staff took their places, Mrs McClusky motioned with her hand and a thousand Grange Hillites sat, let go their breath, shuffled, wriggled and at last were quiet.

'Some, if not all, of you will know what I want to say to you. This term and the next are going to be tough. The shortness of time means we have to work even harder. The future of this school is in the balance. This year, within months, important decisions will be made, decisions about whether or not there will be a Grange Hill.

'You will have heard a lot about falling rolls. This means fewer pupils are coming to our school. Fewer pupils are coming to every school. We are a six-form entry school. We need 180 pupils each year. In 1975 we had 190. By 1985 it will be 118, barely enough for four forms.'

The assembly muttered and shuffled. Mrs McClusky pressed on.

'Now there are four secondary schools in this area – Brookdale, St Mary's High For Girls, Rodney Bennett For Boys, and Grange Hill.'

Mrs McClusky raised her voice.

'It stands to reason that if the number of school children goes down by one third, there will be only enough for three schools not four. One school may well be closed down. Which will it be? You know what will decide. The schools with the best record will survive, those with the exam passes, the best sports performance,' she paused, 'the best public behaviour. And that depends on all of us, all of you. We have to make a good impression and we have the rest of this school year in which to do it.'

She raised her hand to quell another burst of whispering.

'Now I would like you to meet two new members of staff – Mr Golborne, new Head of Studies who will be helping us get those exam passes.'

A tall figure rose and stood by the Head. Broad shouldered, light suited, his face framed in heavy steel-rimmed spectacles. He raised an arm to brush something from his jacket. A dazzling white shirt cuff showed under his sleeve and a gold cuff-link glittered in the light.

'He's dreamy,' said Claire, 'just like Clark Kent.'

'Hey,' whispered Duane, 'look at the other!'

For a second it seemed the school would burst out laughing. By Golborne's side rose a young man, gownless but in faded jeans and crumpled jacket, buttoned on the wrong holes.

'And on Mr Golborne's left is Mr McGuffy,' continued Mrs McClusky, 'who is a probationary teacher. I understand he was once editor of a student magazine, so perhaps his experience will help transform Grange Hill's magazine. We need a new image.'

'Where did they dredge him up?' asked Pogo as loudly as he dared.

'Oh, he's cuddly,' whispered Suzanne 'all arms and legs. We're going to have fun with him.'

'Not the other bloke though,' said Duane. 'He's going to be heavy.'

Mrs McClusky's arm cut off the whispering again.

'That will be all now. Remember, hard work and good behaviour are going to pull this school through.'

Chapter 3

The staff streamed into the staffroom, pulling off their gowns, folding them away into briefcases, or throwing them across chairs.

'I don't know about you, Maureen,' boomed Baxter, as he sorted papers from a pile on a table, 'but I thought the Boss was in great form today. Napoleon addressing the troops could not have been better.'

'Yes, just before the Retreat from Moscow.' Graham Sutcliffe had just come through the doorway, rolling up his gown.

'As bad as that, Graham?' asked Miss Peterson.

He made a face.

'Well, yes, it sounded worse the way she put it to the kids than it did at the staff meeting.'

'Worse, how d'you mean, Graham?' asked Baxter.

'Well, desperate, Geoff, as though this school were first on the list for the chop.'

'Come on, Graham,' Terri Mooney, face flushed, glasses slightly askew, glanced across the now crowded staffroom, her voice rising. Talk around them stopped.

'I mean it,' answered Sutcliffe. 'I have a bad feeling over this whole exercise, this mass hunt after A levels and O levels when a lot of kids are not even in the running for them.'

'They can still try.'

'Great, I was a glorious failure for the Old School.'

'My, Graham, did your porridge go down the wrong way?' Baxter eyed Terri Mooney's frowning face and winked at Miss Peterson.

'I – I think he's right.'

The nervous voice made all the teachers turn to look at McGuffy, the newcomer, his face red as he struggled on. 'I

12

think it is the wrong way to go about it. I think we should be against any school closures at all. If we win the – rat race -- another school loses.'

'Surely not,' a new voice interrupted coolly. Golborne stood in the centre of the room. 'We are in a competition, if you want to call it that, to raise standards for all children, whichever school they go to.'

'Well,' began McGuffy. But he got no further as Mr Keating, the Deputy Head, bustled into the room looking round anxiously.

'Sorry to break this up, but the Head wants to see Subject Heads briefly before we attack the day.'

'What's this?' demanded Miss Lexington. 'I knew nothing about this.'

'Just a quick look at the draft timetable for Spring Tests. The Head wants a flying start.'

'Tests?'

'Yes, I'm afraid we're a bit late getting the timetable out. They'll be in the Head's office.'

'I can let you have a copy, Miss Lexington,' said Golborne, shooting out a gleaming cuff.

'I bet you can,' muttered Graham Sutcliffe.

'I beg your pardon,' said Golborne.

'Nothing.'

Golborne ushered Miss Lexington out of the room and Terri Mooney turned to Graham: 'Well, that was uncalled for.'

He shrugged. She went on: 'What's wrong with you? Why be rude to someone before they've even begun work in the school?'

'Don't you worry,' snapped Sutcliffe. 'Mr Golborne's started work already. I think we are going to have trouble with that gentleman before long.'

'Well, Graham,' said Baxter, 'you can't have an omelette without breaking eggs, and we have to do something drastic to pull Grange Hill up the league table.'

For a second it looked as though Sutcliffe would respond angrily, but Keating intervened. 'Let's try not to panic.

13

We're all over-reacting a little. I myself am pretty sure we'll survive. After all, we do have friends in high places.'

'What friends?'

'Councillor Doyle, our Chairman of Governors, is also Chairman of the Education Committee this year. And when it comes to the crunch . . .'

Miss Peterson's eyebrows rose.

'Hm, if Councillor Doyle is our last hope, then . . .'

'. . . we'd better start looking for new jobs,' said Sutcliffe and marched out of the room, leaving the others staring.

Chapter 4

'Raining again. What a life!'

Trisha Yates swung open the door of the common room and charged in, followed by Cathy Hargreaves. Trisha pulled up suddenly and Cathy barged into her back.

'What was that for?'

From behind the backs of one of the armchairs came a rustling sound and the slightly pink face of Pamela Cartwright appeared.

'What are you up to, Cartwright?'

From the other side of the chair, the long form of Tucker Jenkins uncoiled and transferred itself to the window, whistling and studying the weather with great care.

'Don't be stupid, Trish,' said Cathy, nudging her. 'Can't you see they're revising?' She swung round. 'I bet if we humped this furniture round all sorts of little furry things would fall out.'

'Like what?'

'Like MacMahon and Humphreys. You can't move without tripping over these revision teams.'

'Well,' returned Pamela, 'the Head did say we should put our all into studying, these next three months.'

'What for?' asked Trisha. 'To save this flaming school? You must be joking, Pam. The way Bridget McClusky's been screwing us down these past twelve months, the school's not worth saving. She wants it both ways. We work ourselves into the ground for Grange Hill and get nothing back.'

'We did save the common room,' said Cathy.

Trisha's lip curled.

'Yeah, and lost out on uniforms. No, I reckon this school's going down the tube.'

'And you're just going to let it go?' asked Pam.

Trisha made a face. 'Who's talking? What are you doing,

Miss Cartwright? Looking after number one, and I don't blame you. No, I'll finish off this year on the School Council, help your little brother a bit with the school magazine, then that's my lot. As for studying, where's the point?'

'Oh, come on, Trish, you've got to think about the future. What sort of a job will you get without any O levels?'

'What sort of a job will I get with them? Don't laugh, but the other day I saw this ad in the local rag. Grocer's assistant wanted, minimum two O levels.'

'Trisha's right.' Susi MacMahon and Alan Humphreys had come in. 'Bullet Baxter was outside the gates yesterday with Hopwood, clearing away blokes from the pavement.'

'What blokes?'

'Blokes who left last year.'

'What do they want?'

'Who knows? They've no job, nowhere to go, nothing to do, so they just hang round.'

'That's stupid,' said Cathy, 'last year they couldn't get out of the place fast enough. Now they want back in.'

'They don't know what they want,' said Alan, dropping his bulk into a groaning easy chair.

'Ah, but Mr Humphreys knows what he wants,' jeered Trisha.

'Somebody else does, too,' said Tucker, swinging round from the window.

'Like who?'

'Like your friend and Susi's friend.'

'Who?' Alan sounded suspicious.

'Eddie Carver, who else?'

'Carver, where?'

'Right here, in the school.'

'What's he want?' Alan sounded nervous now.

'Quick rampage through the undergrowth, like at the school camp,' said Tucker, looking cunningly at Susi MacMahon who had gone pale.

'Listen, Tucker,' Alan got up, 'stop stirring it. What is this garbage about Carver?'

'Garbage? No,' answered Tucker, 'Mr Carver has been

seen on the school premises, with Dukeson and Cathy's big brother, Gary, talking to the Head.'

'Oh, I know what that is,' put in Cathy. 'They're asking the Head if school leavers can come back and use the gym and the workshop.'

'What? Old Tom Tom'll never wear that.'

'No, maybe in daytime, there are periods when both are empty.'

'Beat it,' said Alan anxiously. 'Bridget'll never agree to that.'

'You hope,' said Tucker. 'You hope your head's going to stay facing front, don't you?'

Alan suddenly grinned. 'Hey, maybe the idea's not stupid. Bring back all the old boys to use the equipment, like your old pal Booga Benson.'

Now Tucker's face fell.

'Leave off will you, Alan. He's in Remand Centre.'

'You sure?'

Alan went on: 'You know how it's done these days. They let villains come home where they belong and the friendly neighbourhood social worker straightens 'em out. They call it intermediate treatment.'

'Terminal treatment is what that ape needs,' said Tucker.

'I don't think this is funny at all,' said Pamela. 'Let's change the subject.'

'Yeah,' said Tucker, 'let's get back to revision.'

'That's what it's called these days,' Cathy grinned. 'Shall we make up groups of three or four and test each other? Not much time left.'

'Too right,' answered Susi, 'I make it fifty-six days to the first exam.'

'You're joking.'

'I'm not counting weekends. They can have the week but the weekend's my own.'

'I still reckon it's a waste of time,' said Trisha. 'It's all going down the pipe.'

'Oh, Trish,' protested Pamela, 'don't be so miserable. Seriously, do you think they'll close Grange Hill?'

17

'Who knows? Who cares?'

'Somebody knows something. Like Doyle. I was watching him while Bridget was speaking. He had a smirk on his face all the time.'

'So what's new?'

'He had that kind of look that says: "I know something you peasants don't".'

'He probably does. His old man's probably up to something. Question is, what?'

Chapter 5

An early spring morning. 3H stormed in from the cold outside and milled around the classroom, stamping, slapping arms, rubbing hands. It was a tutor period. The tutor, Mr Hopwood, was late and that meant, as usual, pandemonium.

Christopher Stewart banged his desk lid. 'Can you all shut up a minute!'

'Silence, let the monkey speak!' someone yelled. Christopher stood on his chair.

'Matthew Cartwright and I are working on the next issue of the school magazine. If you have any ideas or suggestions . . .'

'How about drop dead?' came from the back of the room.

'Useful suggestions,' Christopher went on.

'How about the Nicker's Guide to the Area by G. Stebson,' said a quiet voice in the crowd at the front of the room.

'I heard that.' Stebson's head turned from the corner of the room where he was chatting to a wiry, pale-faced character called Denny Rees, who had joined the class from another school earlier that term. There was a hush as Gripper's eye roved round the room.

Matthew spoke up: 'If you have any useful ideas – articles, stories, poems, cartoons, just let Stew and me know before Easter. We have to put it all together next term.'

Precious Matthews hurried in from outside, out of breath and pulling a track-suit top off her shoulders. The new lad, Denny, spoke:

'How about Grange Hill chess notes – white to black in three easy moves?'

Precious stopped by her desk. Other people turned.

Precious sent Denny a sharp look.

'What's that supposed to mean?'

His gaze crossed hers insolently.

'Nothing, just a suggestion about the school magazine. Do I have to explain it to new arrivals?'

'Hopwood!' said Pogo Patterson hastily. Christopher climbed down from his chair and the others drifted back to their seats. Mr Hopwood came in frowning and with the barest of good mornings began to hand out duplicated sheets.

'I want these answered. You have,' he looked at his watch, 'thirty minutes at the outside and there are twenty-five questions. That makes . . .'

'One minute twelve seconds per question,' murmured Matthew Cartwright.

'Thank you, Matthew,' returned Hopwood sharply. Matthew started at the tone of the teacher's voice, shrugged and said no more. But Claire Scott's hand went up.

'Sir,' she protested, 'this is supposed to be a tutor period where we sort things out.'

Hopwood glared, then his expression changed.

'Right, Claire, and wrong. We have six tests to complete before term end, and tutor periods are going for a burton.'

'But why, sir?'

'Run up to the summer exams, that's why.'

'But . . .'

'This is a test not a discussion. You have twenty-eight minutes left. Now eyes down, look in.'

The day ground on. No one said much even at break time. Everyone seemed to be weighing up the new regime and what it meant.

Only towards the end of the last period in the afternoon, when 3H were back in their own room and the teacher was out for a few minutes, did conversation really start.

'Hey, Stew,' said Duane, 'how about a special exposure series in the magazine?'

'Like what?'

'Like Grange Hill pupils break down under pressure. Mass suicides in third year.'

'Single homicide if I get another suggestion like that.'

'I'm serious. If they're going on like this we'll all be off our wheels by the end of the month, never mind the year.'

'What do you expect?' Claire spoke across the class. 'You heard Ma McClusky. The school's going all out to win the washing machine.'

'You mean we flog our whatsits off so they don't close the school down. They must be joking.'

'Doesn't it bother you what happens to the school, Duane?' asked Matthew, beginning to put books away in his bag.

'If you want to know, Matthew, the answer is ho ho.'

'What, and have to trek all over the country to Brookdale or wherever?'

'Beat it. They don't do it like that. They don't just close the school down. They just stop taking kids in. The school dies off.'

'What,' said Pogo, 'no more furry little first years?'

'I heard about a school,' said Stew, 'where they just shut it up, shoved the kids into half a dozen other places and flogged the buildings off.'

'How about that?' said Claire. 'Grange Hill for sale.' Pogo picked up the idea.

'What am I bid for . . .?'

'If they sold it by weight, you'd be the best bargain,' said Duane.

'Very witty.' Pogo looked round. 'Anybody coming?' he asked the lad who sat nearest the door.

'Right,' he went on, 'enough fooling around today. Let's get down to serious business.'

He bent down beneath his desk and surfaced holding a size twelve boot, dusty and battered.

'You shouldn't bring your best gear to school, Pogo,' said Claire, 'you'll only get it knocked off.'

'Which end does he wear it, I want to know?'

'Does it matter?'

21

'No joke. Don't you know Douglas Patterson is Britain's first brain donor?'

'Get off.'

'True. But they turned him down after the first test bore.'

'Yeah, solid rock.'

'When you nurdle-brains have finished,' Pogo placed the boot with a thump on the desk top. 'Does anyone want to join?'

'Join what?'

'The Boot Club, stupid.'

'What for?'

'Pay your subscription and you'll find out.'

'I might have known. How much?'

'Twenty-five pence.'

'What d'you get for that?'

Pogo shook his head. 'No information in advance.'

He looked round. 'Anyone interested, meet me outside after.' He looked at Duane. Duane shrugged.

'Anything for a giggle after today.'

Claire nodded.

Christopher shook his head.

'If it's anything like your usual caper, Pogo, you may stuff it.'

'Thank you. But why should I fret? You're the loser.' He looked at Precious.

'Not me, I'm running after school.'

'After Benny Green, you mean.'

Precious turned sharply.

'Who said that?'

'Peterson's coming,' warned the lad at the door.

Miss Peterson looked round the door.

'Now that's strange. Total silence in 3H. What can be going on?'

Chapter 6

A little group stood on the pavement outside the Sports Wear Centre in the High Street. Pogo, Duane, Claire, Tracey and one or two more from 3H. Pogo held a battered shoe-box in his arms.

'Right,' he said. 'The Boot Club is now in session. Are you right, Claire?'

Claire looked flustered, bit her lip.

'I can't do it,' she said. 'I'll make a mess of it, I know. I'll never remember all the names.'

'Course you will,' Duane said encouragingly. 'You've got just the right face for it – innocent like.'

'But the assistant'll sus me out right away.'

'Not him,' said Pogo. 'He's as green as Kermit's bum It'll be a doddle.'

'I don't know.'

'Anyway,' said Pogo, 'you've got to go. Your name came out of the box first.'

Claire hesitated, then a crafty gleam came into Pogo's eye. He looked at Duane.

'I always said we shouldn't have girls in this Club. They chicken out of everything.'

Claire sent him a murderous glance, turned and marched into the shop. The others nudged each other and edged to the shop doorway where they could listen in. Inside, the young, round-faced assistant looked at Claire over his spectacles.

'Can I help you?'

'I'm not sure. It's my brother – his birthday.'

'You want to buy him a present. What have you got in mind?'

'Well, it's a surprise. He's very choosy and I've got to get it right.' Claire started to giggle and the assistant looked at her carefully. She bit her lip and looked round the shop. 'I'm not

23

sure you've even got one. They're very new, just over from Italy. I saw it on the telly.'

'A commercial? Well, we keep up very well with things.'

'No, not a commercial – it's a – puppet programme called the Stranglers.'

'Stranglers?'

'You probably don't watch it. It's on Sunday nights after midnight.'

'How old is your brother?'

'He's about seven . . .' She looked at him. His face brightened. 'Well, you want our children's department.'

Claire looked in the mirror over the counter and saw Pogo in the doorway. He pointed his thumb down. Claire spoke hastily.

'Actually, he's a bit older really, nearly eleven and big for his age.'

'How big?'

'Oh, about five foot nine and, er, ten stone.'

'What's his collar size?'

'Oh, about seventeen?'

'Seventeen?' The assistant took his glasses off, wiped them and looked at the inner door. Through the mirror she could see Pogo and Duane grinning.

'I mean, that's metric. About six or seven.'

'What is he . . . ?'

'Oh, he's quite normal really, but he's very choosy.'

Pogo and Duane were doubling up outside.

The assistant took a deep breath.

'What would you like for your brother? I'll see if we have the size or maybe he could come in and try one on.'

'Oh no,' said Claire, 'it's got to be a surprise.' Her mind raced. She'd forgotten what she had to say. In the mirror there were Duane and Pogo holding their breath. Suddenly she was inspired.

'It's a Kamikaze Sauna Jacket.'

The assistant's mouth fell open.

'A Kamikaze what jacket? I don't . . .'

A broad smile came on Pogo's face. The assistant was

about to say, 'I don't believe it.' That would be one point to Claire, score one all. But instead he went on, 'I don't think I've heard of that – but,' he added quickly, 'I'm sure we can find it. We have hundreds of items in stock – bomber jackets, donkey jackets, flight jackets, Harrington . . .'

'That's it,' said Claire quickly.

'Oh, a Harrington jacket?'

'No, it's like a Harrington jacket.'

'Ah – a . . .'

'Only perhaps a bit more like a Snorkel.'

His eyebrows vanished among his hair. 'Like a Harrington jacket or a Snorkel. It can't . . .'

Outside Pogo was dancing up and down. The assistant turned at the noise and Pogo vanished.

'Now I think of it,' pursued Claire, 'it's more of a Wrangler . . . that's it, it's a sort of a Harrington Snorkel cum Wrangler, with – an attached body warmer.'

The assistant backed slowly away towards the inner door. 'I'll ask. Just a minute.' Claire, alarmed at losing him, shouted, 'They use them for skiing in Saudi Arabia.'

Outside, there was pandemonium. Inside, voices were raised. A middle-aged man came swiftly out into the shop. He pointed at Claire.

'Out!' he said.

Claire became dignified.

'I beg your pardon.'

'You heard. Out.'

'I don't understand. I was only asking for . . .'

'You were wasting our time. Making a nuisance of yourself on purpose.'

From the pavement outside came a muffled burst of applause.

'I'm sure I don't understand,' said Claire demurely.

'Oh yes you do. On your way, madam. If I catch you in here again I'll fetch – ' he paused, 'I'll report you to the school.'

Claire turned.

'I'm sorry you can't supply what I want.'

25

Then she fled. Outside the whole bunch raced down the block. Safely round the corner they stopped. Pogo opened the box and produced the old boot.

'Claire Scott,' he said solemnly. 'I hereby award you this week's Old Boot -- having fulfilled the most stringent conditions -- to have successfully wound up one or more adults without at any moment being rude or in any way badly behaved. Congratulations.'

Chapter 7

Over his four o'clock cup of tea Dan Hopwood nodded at Miss Peterson who lounged deep in an armchair, stocking toes resting on a table top, eyes half closed.

'I think you're right, Maureen. Something is going on in 3H. Something special.'

'What special?' asked Miss Lexington, busy with her briefcase.

Hopwood took a mouthful of tea. 'Oh, just the usual crazy irresponsible kind of scheme that gets them all involved for a week or so, then blows up in their faces, our faces, everybody's faces.'

'Then Saint Dan has to pick up the pieces,' called Baxter jovially from the window. 'There go the last of them. I don't know why you take it so hard, man. Lovely bunch of kids, third year. Salt of the earth.'

'Well, Geoff, you can have too much salt, you know,' said Miss Peterson.

'I don't know,' answered Hopwood, 'sometimes the devil gets into the lot of them. Could be the weather, March winds and all.'

'And it could be the way the pressure's being piled on,' Sutcliffe spoke up from his corner. 'One test after another. the kids are bound to let off steam.'

'Bound to. Come on, Graham,' said Miss Lexington. 'Anyway they're not all in a stupid mood. Young Stewart's bringing out the magazine. Matthew's getting on with the computer project.'

'Ah, the maths genius,' said Baxter. 'What is he, or what are Boris and he up to now?'

'I shouldn't reveal anything, but he's doing some predictions. Population trends to 2000 AD. Seems the slump in population is over. Birth rate is rising two per thousand per year.'

'Ah,' murmured Baxter, 'we know who they are. We've got 'em in the sixth form. Grange Hill's doing its best for the baby boom.'

Hopwood suddenly grinned. 'That may be so, Geoff, but if you're looking to a solution to Grange Hill's problem, that won't help till 1992.'

'Aren't you men just typical.' Terri Mooney had paused in the doorway, arms full of books. 'It's no laughing matter.'

'Quite right, Terri,' said Baxter. 'Just that one gets a little hysterical now and then. Anyway, Dan, there is another bright spot in the third year. Precious Matthews is out training every night. If she does not carry off the decathlon in the Divisional Sports this year, then . . .'

'Yes, I see her every night, jogging along,' grinned Miss Lexington, 'usually about ten yards behind Benny Green.'

'True,' Baxter nodded, 'and I hope there is nothing sexist in that observation. I am putting money on Benny and Precious. One's going to help us beat Brookdale in the District Cup, the other's going to help us get the Sports Shield.'

'Precious worries me a bit,' put in Miss Peterson.

'Oh, why? Level-headed lass, though stroppy on occasion.'

'She seems a bit wound up lately.'

'Someone's winding her up, I think,' remarked Hopwood. 'Who?'

'Not sure, but I think it's that transfer from Rodney Bennett. Name of Denny Rees.'

'Ah, him we know. A junior statesman that – in the making. Enoch Powell of Grange Hill.'

'At the moment, a source of aggro in 3H,' said Dan.

'What, worse than Stebson?'

'Stebson? Do I know him?' asked Miss Lexington.

'Know him?' grinned Baxter. 'How could you not? Once met, never forgotten. Pure bristle. Hundred years ago he'd have had two choices only.'

'Oh, what?'

'Transportation or hanging.'

There was a gulping sound over by the sink as McGuffy, the new teacher, finished his tea.

'You'll excuse me, but I think that's partly the trouble.'

'What might that be, Mr McGuffy?'

'I mean remarks like that. If you expect a kid to turn out like that, what chance has he got?'

'Chance, man? Stebson has taken all his chances. And he will not thank you for your finer feelings so I'd advise you not to show them too freely. Give characters like him a finger and they'll have your arm off.'

McGuffy flushed. 'I happen to disagree . . .'

'Please yourself, mate. You'll change your tune in a few months, if you last out.'

'Thank you very much.' McGuffy slammed down his cup and stormed out of the staffroom, leaving the other teachers staring at each other.

Chapter 8

There was an awkward silence, then Miss Lexington spoke.

'That was a bit uncalled for, Geoff.'

'Uncalled for?' retorted Baxter. 'He's been asking for it since he came here. All this old how's your father. Be nice to them and they'll open up like flowers.'

'Oh, I think you have McGuffy wrong. I don't think he belongs to the flower-garden school,' said Hopwood.

'No?'

'No, he believes in teachers and kids together against a rotten world.'

'There's something in that,' said Miss Peterson.

Baxter snorted. 'Come on, Maureen. You know very well all this revolutionary garbage is just an excuse for not teaching.'

'You are wrong, Geoff. McGuffy is trying hard.'

'But not hard enough. I passed 1G the other day. In an uproar. And there was McGuffy looking like St Francis addressing the vultures, saying: Now, 1G, I don't want to antagonize you but . . .'

'Well,' smiled Maureen, 'what is wrong with that?'

'Well, it's not true, is it? We do want to antagonize them. I mean we want 'em to work and they don't. So we have to antagonize them. Apart from which the kids don't respect him.'

'Really, Geoff. How d'you know?'

'Well, what do they call him?'

'Go on.'

'Scruffy McGuffy.'

'They can be cruel.'

'They can be right. He is scruffy.'

'Oh, come on, he's just not one of the collar-and-tie mob.'

30

'He's scruffy,' insisted Baxter. 'He's one of the Friends of the Earth and he carries a lot of it around on him.'

'Don't be so unkind, Geoff,' chuckled Miss Peterson.

'And he puts his boots on the coffee table.'

'So do you, Geoff.'

'Ah yes, but the heels. He puts the soles on.'

The staffroom rocked with laughter, then in the quiet that followed Graham Sutcliffe said:

'Well, McGuffy may not be a teacher yet, but he'll learn. He's not a menace and he does do his share in the classroom, unlike certain other members of staff.'

Hopwood put down his cup. 'You are not referring by any chance to our respected Head of Studies, Mr Golborne, are you?'

'Head of Studies?' snapped Graham. 'He's a flaming Gauleiter. All he does is go round with his clipboard making work for other people. I bet he's never seen a kid fired in anger in his life.'

'Are you saying he has no classroom experience?'

'I'm saying he's never taught kids who weren't tied down.' He turned to Baxter. 'And the name of his game isn't revolution, it's evolution, turning himself into the highest form of life.'

'I think Graham's got something. I think Keating and the Head had better watch their backs,' said Hopwood.

'And I think Graham is being stupidly biased.' Terri Mooney, coat on, bag packed, stood near the door, her cheeks pink. 'I think exam work needs a boost in this school and that is what it's getting.'

'And I think there is a lot more to school than chalking up A levels. What about the rest of the kids?' answered Sutcliffe.

'You suit yourself.' Miss Mooney slammed the door.

'Don't want to alarm you, Graham old lad, but have you got the car keys, or has Terri? You could find yourself waiting for the bus.'

Baxter chuckled as Graham got to his feet in alarm and charged out. The others began to get their papers together.

31

'Incidentally, have the kids christened Golborne yet?' asked Miss Lexington.

Miss Peterson laughed. 'With those shining cuff-links, how could they not?'

'Let me guess. Something Hollywood. *The Man with the Golden Arm*.'

'Too long.' Maureen shook her head.

'*Goldfinger*.'

'Even better, but not quite there,' said Miss Peterson modestly. 'Another part of the body.'

'Ah,' burst out Baxter. 'I know, Golden – '

'Really, Geoff,' said Mrs Thomas as the staffroom exploded into laughter again.

Chapter 9

'Right,' said Tucker, 'that's it, old Goldenballs has had it.'

'Had what?' Alan looked up from his seat in the common room and watched his mate pace up and down.

'It. Tomorrow we call at the chemist's on the way to school.'

'What for?'

'Rat poison. What else?'

'Big snag,' said Alan. 'How are you going to sign the poison book? With a cross?'

'Ho, ho.'

'Who wants rat poison?' Pamela and Susi appeared in the doorway, coats on and bags over their shoulders.

'Who needs it, you mean? Goldenballs, that's who.'

'Goldenwhat?'

'Golborne.'

'Oh, him. What's wrong with Golborne?' Susi came into the room. Taking Alan's hand she began a pantomime of hauling him up from the seat.

'Golborne's treating us like kids. What do we want supervised revision periods for? We managed all right before.'

'I don't know,' said Susi, thoughtfully. 'I think it's useful having a tutor on hand to check up on things.'

'I think he's right.' Trisha, with Cathy behind her, came into the room. 'What's the good of being upper school if you get treated like first years? We're supposed to be studying for exams. We've got some rights, haven't we?'

'Right on,' said Tucker.

'Hey, that's twice you've agreed with Yates,' said Alan. 'You'd better watch it.' He grinned at Pam who growled and swung her bag low at Alan, making him back hastily away.

'Anyway,' he laughed at Tucker, 'you're just choked because Goldenballs zapped your love-in. You're worried you may find yourself doing some work.'

Tucker jerked his head at Pam and walked to the door. 'As a matter of fact that's my problem, finding a bit of peace and quiet to revise. The flaming telly's on all evening at home and my bedroom's freezing cold.'

'You could sit in our kitchen, Peter,' said Pam, 'and we could test each other.'

'I bet you could,' shrieked Trisha.

'Nah,' said Tucker, 'your mother keeps looking in to see if we want another cup of tea.'

'What's wrong with that?' asked Cathy innocently.

Tucker shook his head at her. 'You can get treatment for your condition, you know.' He looked at Pam. 'Tell you what, see you in the caff, seven o'clock.'

Pamela shrugged.

'Look,' he went on, 'I've got an idea.'

'Yeah, we know,' said Alan. 'The same idea you had yesterday and the day before.'

'Just die out will you. I mean an idea for revising.'

'What's that?' said Pamela doubtfully.

'You really want to know, report to me at nineteen hundred hours.' Tucker walked out, Pamela followed him slowly and Susi and Alan went a few seconds later. Cathy and Trisha looked at one another.

'Bit childish, isn't it?' said Trisha.

'I don't know,' answered Cathy. 'It's rotten if you want to be on your own. I mean where do you go?'

'Humphreys and Susi seem to manage.'

'Manage? Susi's mother lets 'em go in the lounge, but she listens in from the kitchen!'

'I don't know, parents have twisted minds.' Trisha went on: 'Think Pam knows what she's doing with him?'

'Well, she is over sixteen,' said Cathy.

'Yeah, but is he?'

'Course he is.'

'You know what I mean.'

34

'Not sure. But that's her business Don't you worry about Cartwright. She'll pass her O levels, Jenkins or no Jenkins. Wish I could say the same about us, Trish.'

'Wish I cared.'

Chapter 10

Trisha and Cathy stood at the zebra crossing on the High Street. The evenings were getting lighter but the air was still cold. Cathy shivered and pulled her coat more closely around her.

'Coming to the Arndale?'

'What for?'

'Looking for something new.' Cathy paused. 'There's this boy. He does gigs now and then – not really a group, but we might team up. We've been working on some numbers together.'

'Yeah. Is that what they call it now?'

'Oh leave off, Trish. You spoil everything. Are you coming?'

'No, I'm going to the library.'

'What for? Haven't you done enough revising today?'

'I'm going to look up a book on student rights.'

'I thought you'd packed that lark in.'

Trisha shook her head. 'I reckon they're getting away with murder at that school now. You know, I don't believe all that rubbish about closing the school down. I think it's just an excuse for McClusky to turn the place into a concentration camp again.'

'You sound like our Gary.'

'Your Gary, what's that got to do with it?'

'Well, you know him and the others, Dukeson and Eddie Carver went to see Ma McClusky about school leavers using the gym and the workshops when classes weren't in there.'

'So?'

'So she turned them down flat, didn't she?'

'What did they expect?'

'She said there were legal problems, but our Gary reckoned she just didn't trust them.'

Trisha shrugged. 'She doesn't trust anybody.'

'Our Gary says he's going to write a letter to the local paper. Well, Eddie Carver's helping him with it.'

'He'll have to watch it. If he gets a bad name locally, nobody'll give him a job.'

'Who's offering? No, he reckons he'll not sign his name, just make it "name and address supplied".'

'Well, that should put one up Bridget's jumper.'

'Oh, I can't stand here any longer, Trish. You coming?'

'No, you'll just have to pick it yourself. Leave the pink out though.'

'Why?'

'Because it makes 'em think you've just dried out.'

'Ah, the voice of experience. You watch it, Yates. You never know who'll be lurking behind the library stacks. Some of those librarians are devils. All that reading drives 'em mad.'

'See you.'

'See you.'

Trisha crossed the road and walked through the shopping centre into the library complex. It was a new building and she wasn't sure of her way at first. She wandered round the stacks but the more she looked, the more the rows of books confused her. At last she found the card index and began to flip through.

She found 'students', easily. She flipped more cards. 'Grants, see local authorities, finance', then 'see university', 'see polytechnic . . . undergraduate . . . post-graduate'.

'School, see pupils'.

Her eyes began to cross and her head to swim. Half in anger half in desperation she went to the desk. But the librarian was on the phone. After a while a younger woman came and listened patiently to her.

'I'm not sure I've heard of a book on the subject. Have you got an author's name? Can you wait a minute and I'll ask?' But the phone conversation dragged on. Trisha bit her lip and was about to turn away, when someone spoke quietly behind her.

'Excuse me. I couldn't help overhearing. I wonder if you mean the pamphlet on pupils' rights, published a few years ago by the civil liberties people.'

Trisha looked up. She had to. The speaker was tall, bearded, casually dressed. He was older, could have been thirty at least, but he smiled. She could see the librarian was quite taken as well and suddenly felt irritated.

'Well, that will be reference, then. Do you want me to come with you?' The librarian looked half at Trisha, half at the man.

'Don't worry,' he grinned. 'I'll be happy to help, Miss . . .'

'Yates,' mumbled Trisha, turning red and allowing herself to be steered into the reference library.

He turned as they reached the card index: 'Look, if it embarrasses you, just tell me to get lost.'

'No,' protested Trisha. What was he on about? She wasn't a kid.

'O.K. It's just that it looks like a line for a pick up. Let me show you my reference cards, you know.'

For a second a warning bell rang in Trisha's mind. She felt uncomfortable.

Then she felt angry with herself for being stupid. She smiled at him.

'Thanks,' she said, and the two of them began to go through the card index. He showed her how to use it, how to follow through from one reference to another and not get lost. Suddenly Trisha felt she understood. She relaxed more and when their heads knocked together over the drawer, she managed a laugh. But in the end they drew a blank.

'Sorry about that,' he said.

'Not your fault.'

'Are you writing something on student rights for a degree?' he asked as they walked out of the reference room together.

'I'm not at – college,' said Trisha, feeling her face warm up again. 'I'm at . . .'

'Hey, let me guess. You're at Grange Hill.'

She stared at him, suddenly suspicious. He could read her thoughts.

'Just a guess. It was a bit cheeky of me. It's just that I've read a bit about your – place – and the trouble over pupil rights, in the local paper.'

'Huh,' snorted Trisha, 'load of old rubbish that was. Flaming reporters, can't even spell people's names right.'

She caught his eye, embarrassed, amused.

'You're not a reporter, are you?'

He half shook his head. 'Let's say I write, about this and that.'

They'd reached the outer door now. He held it open for her and they stood on the steps outside.

'Look, my name's Hart, Jeremy Hart.' His eye caught hers. 'My friends call me Jim.' He waited.

'Oh, I'm Trisha.'

'Look, er, Trisha. Would you like a coffee? I mean I don't want to keep you, but if you have half an hour.'

An hour later Trisha got home, went straight up to her room and got her books out. As she stared out of the window into the gathering dusk, she thought back on the conversation with Jim. Well, not a conversation really. She'd talked, he'd listened. Usually blokes expected you to listen to them all the time. But he was a funny one. She couldn't make him out.

She went downstairs. Mum and Carol were drinking tea. They looked up and smiled.

'You all right, love?'

'Yes, why not?'

'Well, we haven't heard a peep out of you all evening.'

'She's got a bloke,' said Carol.

'Don't be stupid,' said Trisha, and looked her sister in the eye, hoping her face hadn't changed colour.

Chapter 11

Tucker and Pam looked at one another across the caff table. 'Well,' she demanded, 'what was this idea of yours? I've brought my books, history, biology. What have you brought?'

'Well, I haven't brought my books with me, but,' he said quickly, 'tell you what. I'll test you on your stuff and tomorrow night you can test me on mine.'

'Brilliant, if true. So, what's the idea?'

'It's more a place than an idea.'

'A place?' She looked at him over her coffee cup.

'Just up the road. It's a place – a flat.'

'Peter, what are you on about? What do we want a flat for?'

'It's a place in a block, our kid and his mates are doing up for the council. But just now most of them are empty. It's quite, er, comfortable.'

'Is there any furniture?'

He hesitated. 'Well, there's a mattress and a Lilo on the floor.

Suddenly, she burst out laughing.

'What's so funny?'

'Your finesse, that's all. What's all this business with revision if you just want me up in your brother's sleeping quarters?'

He jumped up, pushing his chair back. Now he was angry.

'Please yourself.' He started to walk out. For a second she just sat there. The street door closed behind him. She leapt up, put down her cup, grabbed up her books and rushed out. The pavement was empty. She looked this way and that, suddenly feeling silly. Someone tapped her shoulder.

'Excuse me, madam, you can't wait here. People get the wrong impression.'

It was Tucker. He had hidden at the side of the door.

'Peter, you maniac.' She looked at him. 'Come on, show me this hideout.'

They crossed the road and he pointed the way into a side street. He didn't take her arm, but rested his arm on her shoulder. It made him feel more in control. She let him steer her along one pavement, then another. She stopped.

'Let me guess. You're taking me back to school?'

He grinned in the half darkness. 'As a matter of fact it overlooks Grange Hill.'

'You mean that block on the corner? But that's nearly new.'

'Was. Been done over so badly no families would stay in it. The council's getting it done up and letting it out to single people. Here we are.'

They stopped and looked up. The block loomed over them in the dusk and behind it was the familiar shape of the school.

'Hey, we'll be right on top of the school.'

'Right. From the window with binoculars you can see right up Tom Tom's left nostril. Be surprised what he gets up to at night.'

'I don't believe you, Peter.'

'Suit yourself. Come on.' He led the way through the swing doors. They were battered and needed a good shove to open. Inside, the passage smelt of damp and cats.

'No lift.'

'You could have fooled me.'

They climbed the stairs.

The stairway was completely dark and she held on to his jacket as they climbed.

'Peter, has this flat any lighting?'

He was silent a minute.

'Peter, I'm turning round right now.'

'Course it has.'

'How much further?'

'Two more flights.'

They paused by the door. From the side of the landing came a powerful blast of cold air through a broken window

41

Tucker felt in his pocket. Pamela touched the door. It moved.

'Hey, it's open,' she whispered.

'Can't be.'

''Tis.' She pushed it open.

'Funny, our kid must have forgotten. He'd leave his head if it wasn't screwed on. Come on.' He stepped inside and groped along the wall. Then he stopped so that she bumped into him.

'What's that?'

He put a hand on her arm. From the room inside came a murmuring and scuffling. Tucker moved swiftly forward, reached round the inner door jamb and switched on the lights.

A single bulb in the ceiling came to life, giving off a pale light, enough to show two people sitting sheepishly on a makeshift settee of piled up mattresses.

'Alan,' said Tucker.

'Susi,' said Pam.

'What are you doing here?' all four said together.

Chapter 12

Tucker stared at Alan and Susi as they slowly struggled up from the mattresses.

'Go on,' he jeered. 'Tell me you were revising.'

Alan pointed down. The mattresses were strewn with books and papers.

'We were.'

'Pull the other, it's got bells on.'

'We were.' Susi was indignant.

'Didn't you get eye strain in the dark?'

'We had the lights on. Then we heard someone outside and we switched off. It's true.' Alan went over to the attack.

'And what're you doing here? You haven't even got your books.'

Tucker turned and pointed to the pile of books under Pamela's arm.

'Course we have.'

The four of them looked at each other and started to laugh. Then stopped.

'How did you get the key?' asked Tucker and Alan both at once.

'I got it from our kid,' said Tucker.

Alan pushed out his lower lip. 'I got it from – a bloke.'

Tucker stared. 'Come on. How much?'

'A oner.'

'You're crazy. Hey! Our kid and his mates must be flogging these keys all over the place.'

Alan shook his head. 'No, I've got to give it back to him.'

'You want your bumps feeling. A quid!'

'Anyway, what are we going to do now?' asked Susi.

'We'll have to share his key, won't we?' said Alan.

'Well, we could,' said Tucker, 'fifty pence each.'

'Peter.' Pamela pushed her elbow into Tucker's ribs. 'Stop

43

it. Anyway, I don't fancy this as a study centre.' she said.

'Nor me,' said Susi.

'Let's go to the chippy,' said Alan.

'First good idea you've had this year,' said Tucker.

The four of them filed out on to the landing and Tucker slammed the door of the flat. Cautiously they began to go down the stairs, Alan in the lead. On the second landing he paused.

'What's that?'

'Ah, nothing,' said Tucker.

'Yes, there was,' put in Susi. 'There's someone coming up the stairs.'

'Let's go back.'

'Beat it.' Tucker listened. 'There's only two of them. Come on.' He pressed on, reluctantly followed by the others. They rounded the corner of the next landing and stopped short, all blinded for a moment by the light from a powerful torch. Dimly behind the glare they could see two figures.

Then came a voice, familiar, unmistakable.

'Look who's here! Isn't that lucky now? Jenkins the nark and his bit and Fatty Humphreys. That's made my evening.'

The light from the torch came nearer. Tucker shaded his eyes.

'Oh, he's worried, isn't he? So he should be. I'd be worried if I was him.'

It was Booga Benson and friend.

Chapter 13

For a second Tucker thought of jumping Benson and escaping down the stairs. But Benson had moved away from the edge of the steps and stood with his back to the outer wall. The torch played up and down.

'I wonder what they've all been up to?' Benson turned to his mate. 'Shall we have a guess?' His friend said nothing. He seemed to be trying to keep behind the torch beam. Benson chuckled.

'Tell you what. Let's keep the birds back, and push these two down the stairs.'

Alan pushed in front.

'Listen, Benson, you . . .'

'Oh, what are we going to do about it then?' Benson took Alan's jacket in his hand and fingered it. 'Maybe my mate can have you. I want Jenkins.' He turned back to Tucker. 'I bet you can still feel it in your ribs, where I gave it to you last time. You're going to wish I'd finished it off then.'

Tucker's stomach chilled. Then he braced himself. Whatever happened he was not going to let Benson work him over again. But what he'd do and how, his mind wouldn't tell him. It had seized up.

Suddenly there were more footsteps from below. Three more figures appeared on the landing. The torch swung round. Now it was Ala..'s turn to go cold in his innards. The first figure was Eddie Carver. He heard Susi draw a quick breath behind him. This was the night of the long knives all right. If Benson owed Tucker for blowing the whistle on him over smashing up the school, then Carver owed Susi and him for that fight in the woods at school camp. Carver still had the mark on his skull where Susi had felled him with a half brick.

The small landing was crowded. Carver's two friends

stood a pace or two behind him on the stairs. They couldn't even make a break for it, thought Alan desperately.

Carver spoke. His voice was calm, easy.

'Which flat are you using, Jenkins?'

'The – top one.'

'That's all right then. I thought we'd been screwed for a minute. We're somewhere else.' He came closer. 'You stick to your place, we'll stick to ours. You haven't seen us, we haven't seen you. O.K.?'

His eyes rested for a moment on Susi, then on Alan. But he said nothing more, but turned to Benson and jerked his head towards the upper stairway.

Benson hesitated.

'Come on.'

The five pushed past along the landing and their footsteps sounded on the stairs above. Higher up, a door creaked open and slammed. There was silence except for their breathing. Then Susi said:

'I feel sick.'

Tucker's head felt light with relief.

'What was all that about?'

'Don't know and don't want to know,' said Alan. 'Come on, let's go and eat.'

Tucker slapped him on the shoulder. 'Look, you three go on. I'm going back.'

'You're out of your box,' protested Alan.

'Listen, mate. I'm just going to have a quick ear at the door. If there's any aggro I can come down these stairs faster than any of those apes. You lot wait at the bottom.'

Tucker sneaked back up the stairs. He listened at the first door. Nothing. The place was empty. Up another flight. He paused again. This time he heard voices. Loud voices. They were rowing over something. He pressed his ear to the door and picked up Booga Benson's voice.

'Listen, Eddie. What d'you want to get in my way for? I owe Jenkins.'

'No, you listen, Benson. If you weren't bricked up inside,

'you'd understand. You bust Jenkins up and you'll be back inside, really inside this time. That matters – a bit. What really does matter is they'd be on to us.'

Carver's voice grew quieter.

'I thought it was clear. This side of the business is low profile. Do you understand low profile, Noddy? That means you don't do, you don't say, you don't breathe in or out unless I say. Get it? You cock this lot up and I'll personally shop you myself.'

There was silence for a second or two. Then the voices began again, but further away. Tucker could hear no more.

Whistling softly between his teeth, he slid quietly down the stairs to catch up with the others.

Five minutes later they were strolling along the High Street. But, though they did not know it, they were being watched.

Chapter 14

Sergeant Harris, lean, smart and grey-haired, strode up the police station steps, in through the office, nodding to the duty man who was getting ready to go, and up into the charge room. There, seated by the window which overlooked the main street, were two men, drinking tea and silently watching the shifting scene outside. One was in uniform, jacket open, fat and white-haired, the other in plain clothes, thin, sad-faced and balding. Sergeant Harris looked at them for a second.

'What a sight for sore eyes. Jacks and Wallies sitting side by side, sharing the cup that cheers but not inebriates. And if they can get on together, why cannot Reagan and Brezhnev manage it? I ask.'

The fat man, PC Alf Benson, half turned his head and said:

'There might be one in the pot, Sarge.'

Harris picked up the pot and poured himself a cup.

'If there were not, Constable, that would be a misdemeanour at the very least.'

He turned to the plain-clothes man.

'Aren't we speaking tonight, Charlie?'

Detective-Constable Taylor cleared his throat.

'I said "good evening", Sarge.'

'Ah, I forgot – the whispering baritone. Why don't you get those tubes fixed? All that waiting on draughty corners, that's what does it.' He nodded to the window. 'What's new?'

PC Benson grinned. 'Nothing, Sarge. Like a good TV series. Nothing happening and the same familiar faces appearing and reappearing.' He gestured to the window and the sergeant looked across the road.

A group of young blokes and girls were fooling around under the street lamps.

'Let me guess. Graduates of Grange Hill Academy for Young Gents and Ladies. Do I know the dark-haired one?'

Charlie shook his head. 'Nah, Sarge, just a family likeness. That's the younger Jenkins. You know his older brother. The others are very respectable.'

'Apart from which,' added Benson, 'they're not graduating till next year.'

'Ah yes, to swell the ranks of the Great Unemployed.'

'Hope not,' said Charlie, 'my boy's leaving next year. Besides,' he added, 'we've got enough with the present lot on the social. Too much time, not enough money and no occupation at all.'

'Ah,' said Benson, 'but some of them are training hard.'

'For example?'

'There's one just back from holiday camp.'

'Ah, remand centre, you mean, Alf. You're a little unfair on our reformed criminal procedure, don't you think?'

Charlie grinned. 'Alf's the man who invented the short sharp shock, Sarge.'

'You mean Alf's answer is fill the hospitals and empty the prisons.'

'I'm not staying here to be insulted,' rumbled Benson. 'I'm for the wide, wide world. Where's my hat?' He reached under the chair for his helmet and ambled to the door, buttoning his jacket. He turned.

'But that bloke I mentioned wants watching. He's doing nothing now but he's only waiting for somebody to point him in the right direction and he'll go off bang.'

The door closed and Sergeant Harris looked at the plain-clothes man.

'What's that all about, Charlie?'

Charlie grinned mournfully.

'Young bloke called Benson, Booga Benson. Sent away as it happens, for going over that lad Jenkins at school. Very dodgey.'

'Benson? Not some relation of our Alf's?'

'Well, Alf does ride a bike you know. Nah, no relation.

49

Just coincidence. Mind you, they'd even nick your name round here.'

Sergeant Harris drank his tea slowly.

'All the same, Charlie. You must admit, given we've got all these kids on the dole, it's been remarkably quiet on the manor. Bit of pushing and shoving outside school gates, old scores and that, but nothing really trying.'

'That's the worrying thing, Sarge.' answered Charlie. 'It's too quiet. There are half-a-dozen herberts who are so quiet it's indecent. They *ought* to be up to something.'

'Don't look a gift horse in the mouth, man.'

Charlie put down his cup and stood up.

'Not a gift horse, Sarge. Somebody is up to something. When they're doing I'm happier, because mostly it's something stupid. When they're not doing, they're thinking and that could be worse.'

'You mean someone's got 'em on the back plate for some foul purpose.'

Charlie shook his head. 'Can't be sure. There's one bloke I've got my eye on. Likely lad called Carver. Good name. I think he has ambitions.'

'What, a new firm?'

'Dunno, could be nastier.'

'What – politics? The Castro of Grange Hill, eh?'

'You're about one hundred and eighty degrees out. Sarge.'

'Oh, that way, Enoch for King, eh?'

Charlie nodded.

'Don't say that, squire. The last thing we want is Superintendent Oakley to bring in the Society for Perfect Gentlemen.'

He looked out again.

'So what else is new at Grange Hill? Pity if they closed that University of Life down, eh, Charlie? Half the meaning would go from our lives.'

'Talking about politics, Sarge, there's a new teacher there. bit of a hippy type, without the long hair. Irish name. spends a lot of time in the pub round Broadwood.'

'That's a wide net, Charlie, Irish blokes drinking in pubs.'

'He does his boozing with Riordan and the stewards of the building site there. Always spouting.'

'Ah, the Trotsky of Tipperary, eh?'

'Nah, just very intense, if you know what I mean. The blokes play him up something rotten, wind him up to see what he'll say next.'

'You're right, Charlie,' said Harris. 'This window is better than the TV. Here come the joggers.'

'Which ones?'

'The short brown one and the long black one.'

'Oh, the lad and the girl?' Charlie looked out of the window. 'There they go. She's always ten yards behind him.'

'Pacing?'

'To be honest I don't think he likes her following him, but he can't shake her off.'

'True devotion. Some of us have that fatal fascination for women. Still, jogging's not our department.'

'No, but I tell you what might be, Sarge, since we're still on Grange Hill.'

'What?'

'Just a bubble from one or two of the shops. Bit of nuisance from some of the thirteen-year-olds.'

'Not on the rob again?'

Charlie shook his head.

'Not as far as I can make out. Don't know what they're up to. But they're up to something.'

Chapter 15

'Order of the Boot?' said Baxter. 'What next, Oh Lord? Tell me, Maureen, why do we have to have a third year? Why can't that age group be abolished? Or better still, sent to training camp.'

'Aha,' said Dan Hopwood, 'cold baths and short sharp shocks. You are an old reactionary, Geoff, McGuffy was quite right.'

'Oh, him? How is he getting on now? Since he hasn't got the next train back to Hampstead, I take it he is getting on.'

'He's doing all right,' said Miss Peterson. 'In fact, I'm sorry to tell you this, Geoff, but the kids seem to like McGuffy.'

'I'm not sure if they *like* him, yet,' said Hopwood. 'Right now they feel sorry for him.'

'I think there's more to it,' put in Sutcliffe. 'I think they see him as one of them. They really believe he's on their side.'

'So, while they're busy winding up the adult world and awarding themselves points for doing it, young Scruffy goes scot-free.'

'No, that I wouldn't say,' answered Graham. 'I think maybe they're giving him a rough ride, but he still likes them and they like him.'

'True,' put in Maureen. 'The girls think he's cuddly, all arms and legs. Don't look disgusted, Geoff. I'm afraid that's more than they're prepared to say about Mr Golborne.'

'Ah, the renowned Goldenballs. Haven't seen him at work with the Great Multitude yet.'

'You're not likely to,' said Sutcliffe. 'His speciality is making work for other people.' He looked round.

'All right, Graham,' said Miss Peterson, 'Terri's not around. You may discuss Mr Golborne freely, short of slander that is.'

Sutcliffe grinned wryly. 'He's got under my skin all right – and other people's too. He's split the staff down the middle.'

'Well, Graham, some of us think he has brought a much needed touch of order to exam preparation, and Grange Hill needs that,' said Mrs Thomas quietly from her corner.

'Exam-taking isn't everything,' answered Sutcliffe. 'But what gets me is all this paper work. Tests, assessments, percentages, endless meetings. Look around this room. Most of us are lugging home more papers than ever, and for what? So the school can compete in some game where we don't even know the rules and we'll only find out the score when we know we're out of the game.'

'So you still think it's all up with Grange Hill, Graham? Even with the renowned Councillor Doyle batting for us? I'm told that at the last governors' meeting he made quite a speech – "Every confidence in Grange Hill, do all in my power to help." And he is a power in the land, and after the Spring Elections I suspect he'll have even more power.'

'Funny thing is,' said Miss Peterson, 'while Doyle the father makes reassuring noises, Doyle the son is going about with an oily smile on his face.'

'At least he's not trying to make our lives miserable, Maureen,' said Hopwood.

'I know. Exemplary behaviour. He seems to be just waiting for everything to fall into a big hole in the ground so he can have the last laugh.'

'Maybe. Still, all's quiet on that front now. Jenkins, Humphreys and the rest are all busy studying.'

'Or pursuing the Misses Cartwright and MacMahon.'

'Or both.'

'No harm in that.'

'You hope.'

'Don't be a spoilsport, Geoff. Does nothing please you?'

'Nothing will,' answered Baxter, 'until we have the District Championship and the Divisional Sports Shield in the bag.'

'And how are your stars doing, Benny and Precious?'

'Couldn't be better. I had a bad moment when Mr Green

came round and read me the Riot Act because Benny was neglecting his studies.'

'Oh dear.'

'Not true, in fact. Benny's working hard at both and once the deciding match is over, he'll be studying harder. I've every confidence in Benny.' He turned to Hopwood.

'How's Precious getting on?'

Hopwood shrugged. 'Little easier. This lad Denny Rees gives her a hard time now and then.'

'Correction, gives everyone a hard time.'

'But very polite and well behaved, Mr Rees. Could be a Boot Club member.'

'Not he, bigger stakes. He came in last week with a badge, "I'm dreaming of a White Christmas". I told him to take it off, but next day he was wearing red, white and blue socks.'

'That was for my benefit,' said Miss Peterson. 'What did you do?'

'What could I? Told him if he wanted to wrap the Union Jack round his sweaty feet, that was his business.'

'He's beginning to get to you, Dan.'

'Hope not. Life's too short. But I think he does get to Precious, though.'

'She'll survive. Still training hard?'

'Yes, still tailing Benny Green on the jogging circuit.'

'Don't think Benny cares for that.'

'No harm in it, though.'

'Let's hope not. Hope springs eternal.' Baxter gathered his gear together. 'When I was McGuffy's age I thought life was my oyster. Now I'm just hoping to get through this school year. Let's go home.'

Chapter 16

One evening near the end of term just after school, across the main road, in one of the side streets, Precious Matthews set out for her evening jog. She ran easily, her long legs covering the ground in regular strides, head up, hair bobbing. People saw her passing and grinned. One or two passed remarks but she ignored them. You had to try and cut some things out. Miss Peterson had told her that if you reacted to everything people said, or everything you thought they said, you'd be so wound up, you'd stop breathing.

She swung on to the High Road, slowing her pace. She didn't want to tread too close on Benny Green. He liked to run on his own. She guessed he might be a bit annoyed at her tailing him, but she shrugged. Benny was good. He had nerve.

Ahead the pavement was clear save for a walking couple. Funny. No Benny. On into the shopping centre she ran, looking around her. But her front runner was nowhere to be seen.

Crossing at the zebra, she set course for the gardens and the park. She'd make a quick circuit and then home. Benny must be sick. As she rounded a massive bush in the gardens, there he was, standing in her path, in his running gear. She slowed up, smiled.

'Hi.'

'Look, kid,' Benny seemed annoyed and embarrassed. 'You have to tail me like this?'

'What's wrong with it?'

'Looks stupid, that's what. Can't you go another way?'

'This is the best route, you know it is.'

He did.

'Can't you start the other way round?'

She bit her lip. He looked at her.

'Hey, what's wrong?'

She looked down, shifted her feet.

'Don't like running quite on my own.'

He let out a breath.

'Ah . . .' Then he stopped, as if thinking of something. He looked past her.

'O.K. Let's run together.'

Back in school Matthew Cartwright and Christopher Stewart faced one another across a paper-strewn table in the library. Christopher was put out, but with one eye on the librarian, he spoke in a whisper. That made him seem even more angry.

'Look, mate, all I can say is thanks very much.'

'What's that mean?'

'I mean for all the help you're giving me on this school magazine.'

'I've been busy with my computer project.'

'Yeah, messing about with Boris, while I'm slaving over a hot magazine.'

'But I thought you had enough stuff already.'

'Stuff? Of course I have, but it's no good.'

'A message from the Head, saying what she says in Assembly every two weeks. A bundle of poems. An Oh-wasn't-it-lovely story about the trip to France . . .'

'Sounds fair enough.'

'Oh, come on, Matthew. The school's on its last legs and we're fooling around with this kind of parish-magazine stuff.'

'Hasn't old Scruffy done anything?'

'He's full of ideas, but they don't seem to come to anything.'

'How about: "Passing Exams in Three Easy Lessons" by Prof Goldenballs?'

Christopher stood up, his voice rising. The librarian turned. He sat down and hissed at Matthew.

'Don't waste my time, mate.'

Matthew suddenly grinned.

'Stew, I'm sorry. I'll try and think of something, promise.'

56

He paused. 'Listen, I'm not being funny, but would you like to see what I've been up to with Boris?'

Christopher's eyes rolled.

'If you're sure it's decent.'

'Well, it's sort of sensational.'

'Get off – string of figures.'

'True, but statistics can reveal or conceal.'

'Don't be a bighead.'

'I'm serious. Are you coming?'

Reluctantly, Christopher gathered together his papers and stowed them in his bag. Matthew was already at the door.

Fastening the bag, Christopher followed him down the passage to the room where the computer was kept.

They stopped in front of it.

'Well, come on. Do the old flashing lights and revolving tapes bit, then.'

Matthew shook his head. 'Can't do that. Not supposed to switch it on unless Lexi's here.'

He took a file from his bag and opened it, unfolding a series of print-out sheets. Christopher's eyes boggled at the columns of figures, the code words, the short mysterious sentences.

'Great. Now give me a rest. Show me something boring.'

Matthew looked at him, eyebrows raised.

'All right, Stew. Joke over. These figures show what the population of England and Wales is going to be each year until 2000. They estimate how many per thousand the live birth rate will be. How many boys, how many girls.'

'Why does that matter?'

'More boys means fewer babies.'

'Why?'

'Boys don't get pregnant, do they?'

'That's a blessing.'

'Shut up, Stew, will you. These figures show the number of kids there could be in the schools each year.' Matthew opened a drawer and pulled out a sheaf of graph papers and spread them out on the top of the machine.

'See that line. 1964, 1970, 1976, 1977, number of school kids going down all the time.'

'McClusky told us. Who needs Boris?'

'Now look, 1978, the line starts going up, still going up in 1981. Question is, how far does it go up in the future, or does it come down again?'

Matthew waved another sheet.

'This is kids coming to Grange Hill. 1975 – 190, 1981 – down to 142. By 1988, it might be 110 or less. Now look,' he picked up another sheet of graph paper.

'What are the crossed lines for?' asked Christopher.

'That's the prediction. One line says by 1996 we'll still only have 135. The other says we'll have 180 or more.'

'Why two figures?'

'There could be three or four. What happens to the birth rate in the future is guesswork. So far, they've guessed very badly.'

'So?'

'So the real point is this. The thing is when they talk about Grange Hill and the future, they're guessing. But they only use one figure. The lowest.'

'Hey, and if they're wrong, they could have wiped the school out for nothing and have to build a new one?'

Christopher thought a minute.

'Suppose they don't realize? They could be in lumber.'

'I think they do.'

'You what?'

'I think they know. I think they want the school closed down anyway. Why give themselves a hard time worrying about the future?'

'It's a fiddle?'

'Sort of.'

'What are you doing with all these figures now, Matthew?'

'I've got to put them together, check, re-check, then show it all to Lexi.'

'Can you give me those figures again?'

'What for, Stew?'

'I've just had an idea.'

Christopher and Matthew switched off the lights in the computer room and went out.

Meanwhile, over at the Arndale, Duane was winning his Boot in the model shop.

An assistant was looking through the stock for a Mark Six Cobra Mustang jet fighter, with caterpillar tracks and wall-to-wall carpeting.

Chapter 17

One morning, the Head called in Mr Keating.

'Have you seen these?' she asked.

He looked at the two newspaper cuttings pasted on to foolscap and shook his head.

'Letters in the local paper. I spoke too soon when I said they seem to be giving us a clear run this year.'

She pointed to the paper.

'One's a letter about my refusing to let the school leavers use the gym and workshop. They must know my problems. My hands aren't free. There's no signature, but it could only be written by one of the ex-pupils who came to see me.'

He clicked his tongue.

'It's a bit strong. But they obviously feel bitter about the whole situation.'

'Oh, it's not that I mind. It is this phrase the paper has pulled out for the headline. "Does Grange Hill Care?" It's so unfair. It's cheap and nasty.'

'Local paper trying the Fleet Street touch, I'm afraid, Head. What about the other one?'

'Oh, that one. Pure filth. "Why close Grange Hill? Keep it open for immigrants and let our kids go to decent schools."'

'This one's signed, Head.'

'Yes, look at it. I. M. WHITE.'

'The address is real enough.'

'It isn't. I've had it checked by the Bursar. That number in Kettlewell Street is empty, due for demolition.'

'An old trick. But a nasty one.'

'Someone has got it in for Grange Hill.'

Keating shook his head. 'I think you are over-reacting. This is the first unfavourable mention we've had in the local press for some time.'

'Good Lord, the way you put that it sounds terrible.' She grinned, then was serious again.

'I think there is more to follow. I feel it in my bones. And goodness knows we are doing all we can for the school's image.'

'True, Mrs McClusky, true.'

Mrs McClusky paced to the window, then back to the desk, sat down, thrust the newspaper cuttings into a file and looked up.

'And if that were not enough, I have had a phone call from one of the local shops today. Some of our third years have started a systematic campaign of irritating the shop-keepers.'

'Campaign?'

'So he claims. Some kind of bet or dare – a club.'

Keating smiled: 'Ah, I've heard of this. Called the Boot Club. Have they actually done anything wrong?'

'Apparently not. They're perfectly polite. That seems to upset people even more. Well, we shall have to do something about it. I think I shall talk to school about it next week.'

'You don't think you've been overdoing the Riot Act a bit lately?'

'I beg your pardon.'

Keating hesitated.

'Can I be frank?'

She spread out her hands.

'I think the school is being driven a little too hard on too tight a rein. This may do good, but it also creates tension, you know, and the third year is the leaky valve. It usually blows first. All kinds of silliness, letting off steam. Then . . .' he paused.

'The staff have been feeling the strain, too,' Keating went on.

'Hah,' the Head snorted, 'tell me something new. I'm feeling the strain. The whole situation's a strain. That's no excuse.'

'I mean,' Keating said, 'all the extra paper work, all the

reporting, assessment, repeated testing. It does seem to have multiplied in the past term.'

'But that is just what I brought Golborne in for, to tighten up on things.'

'That's not quite the word the staff are using.'

'Oh, and what word are they using? Come on.'

'Ah – screwing.'

She slammed her hand on the desk.

'How infantile! Anyway, let's concentrate on the kids themselves. You don't favour any move over this – Boot Club – just yet?'

'No. We should wait and see. If they go over the mark, then would be the time. But probably, like all the crazes, this one will just die out.'

Chapter 18

Saturday morning. Fine and sunny at last. Relaxed and out of uniform the Boot Club gathered on the Parade, outside the hairdressers'.

'It's about time,' said Pogo, 'that the President showed you rank and filers how it is really done. Time for a touch of class.' He polished his nails on his sweat-shirt. Duane yawned loudly.

'I can't wait. After all, everyone else has had a go. Some of us quite brilliantly, I must admit.'

'Yes,' added Claire, 'I can't see that there are any new tricks in the bag.'

Pogo waved his hand.

'So far, what have we seen? Merely the horses' doovers. This time it is the piece de resistance.'

'Oh well, if you're going to be vulgar, I'm going home,' said Tracey.

'Get on with it, Pogo,' urged Claire. 'All this blow and no show is making me tired.'

'Too right,' said Duane. 'I think it's all mouth. He's been hanging back because he just hasn't got the bot . . .'

'Sheer envy,' Pogo dug Duane in the ribs. 'Now watch this.'

'Where are you going?'

'In here.'

'What, Luigi's? Never! I thought you took yours off at night and hung it in the wardrobe.'

Pogo stroked his ginger locks. 'You are about to see the ultimate in wind-ups. When he takes off there will be a hole in the ceiling. What's more, I want you to sit in with me, you could learn a lot. Call it a master class.'

'Huh. I think it's a load of rubbish. Anyway, it's not fair.'

63

pointed out Claire. 'You know Luigi's English isn't all that good. You're taking advantage.'

'Yeah, Pogo. You kept the easy one till last.'

'Look, do you apprentices want to see how it is done or don't you?'

Claire shrugged. 'What have we got to lose?'

They filed into the shop. Luigi was busy polishing the bald dome of an old age pensioner. He flourished the apron, bowed and presented the customer with a tissue.

'See you soon, eh?'

'Next year, I expect,' said the old man, winked at the Boot Club and shuffled out, with Luigi brushing him down as he went.

'Now, sir, madam, what shall it be?'

'Our little brother wants a pudding cut,' said Duane quickly.

'Pudding cut. That one I don't know.' Luigi spread out his apron like a bullfighter in the ring. 'Anyway, sit down and let's talk.'

Pogo glared at Duane and sat in the chair, while Luigi tucked the apron under his chin, then touched the flowing locks.

'That's – very nice. Make a nice natural wig. Can I make you an offer, sir?'

He winked at Claire who collapsed into giggles. Duane grabbed a copy of the *Sun* from a chair and pretended to be looking at page three. There was a small silence. Luigi waited. Then Pogo spoke.

'I'd like a Duck's Elbow, please.'

'Eh? That's a new one, on me.'

Luigi looked up at the ceiling. 'Wait a minute.' He went across to the back of the room and pulled open a drawer then returned flipping through the pages of an old magazine.

'Here we are. Was once very popular. Teddy Boys all had them. But that's not Duck's Elbow. That's – Duck's Arse.'

Claire shrieked. Duane collapsed under his newspaper. Tracey held her stomach and groaned.

'No, no,' protested Pogo. 'My mum'd kill me if I had

anything rude like that. No, a Duck's Elbow is something new.'

Luigi put his head on one side and picked up his scissors.

'O.K. We live and we learn. You tell me.'

'A Duck's Elbow is a sort of combination – it's part a quarter-inch clip, a moderate skin, then a Kojak strip over the crown and the left-hand side is Teddy-boy style with a peak.'

Luigi tapped his teeth. Duane and the others held their breath. Luigi fiddled with the back of the chair.

'Hm, hm, hm, and hm. I think – I got it.'

With the speed of light, he slipped the chair into the shaving position, leaving Pogo spreadeagled. Then for a few seconds, his fingers worked up into a blur, the scissors clicked like a machine-gun and ginger hair flew like feathers at a chicken plucking. Claire's giggles ended in a choke, Duane put down his paper and stared in horror and Tracey put her hand to her mouth.

Above Pogo's strangled grunts now rose the whir of the clipper. With iron hand, Luigi swung the shorn head this way and that. Then with a cry of 'Presto', he hurled the chair back into the upright position, whipped off the cloth and said to the stupefied Pogo, 'How you like it? Is it – right?'

Trembling with shock, looking like an Apache brave's nightmare, Pogo clambered from the chair. Before the other three could get up he had vanished from the shop.

Duane rose from his chair.

'I'm sorry. He seems to have gone. How much do we owe you?'

Luigi waved his hand.

'That one – was on the house.'

Chapter 19

Dear Diary Person,

So much to tell. Never a dull moment at Grange Hill, that's for sure.

I told you about my classmate Samuel, or Zammo. Real little egg. Always fights his way out of trouble. This time he was *too* smart. He had the two nasties of the third after him – Gripper Stebson and one Denny Rees. They had him cornered and were just about to liquidize him, when up came Alan Humphreys. He's the sort of Robin Hood of Upper School and he tapped their heads together. So far, so good, but Zammo should watch it. The good guys will not always be around.

So, what next? Annette and Jonah. She is just *wild*. She dared him to a strip-snap session in the stationery cupboard. Not strip poker, you note, since the cupboard only holds two. At first all the cards came Jonah's way. But she was cute and took off one shoe lace, then the other.

Then her luck changed and what do you know? Miss Mooney arrived. Annette moved out – but on wheels, and there was Jonah doing a lot of explaining.

More crazy behaviour. The Boot Club has run on to the rocks. First Douglas Patterson came to school with his hair in a mess, everything from Teddy Boy to skinhead. They called it a Duck's Elbow and guess what? Of course. Twenty boys came to school last week with the same. They looked ghastly.

So, what then? Mrs McClusky bans the Boot Club and all returns to peace and quiet.

Meanwhile outside the school gates there are gangs of kids, who should really be in work, if they had jobs. Sometimes there's pushing and shoving. One or two are really nasty. They come from the other side of town and their game is jostling – or so they call it – black kids and teachers

They made one mistake. They tried it on Miss Peterson. our judo freak. She put an arm round this big guy's neck – only it was his own arm. Painful. She was going to wheel him somewhere when he got loose and made dust trails for home.

You know, I begin to like this school. Never a dull moment.

Belinda

Chapter 20

'Maureen.'

Miss Peterson, crossing the staffroom on her way to take a class, turned at the sound of Hopwood's voice.

'Yes, Dan. Is it urgent? I'm late as it is.'

'Sorry, but it is rather important.'

'O.K.' She halted in her stride. 'What is it?'

'It's Precious.'

'Oh dear. What's gone wrong now?'

He made a face.

'In a way she did nothing I wouldn't have done myself.'

'Now that's intriguing. Tell me more.'

'She got into a fight just before break.'

'Never. She gets on pretty well with the other girls.'

'Oh no. It was Denny Rees.'

'Ah. Serious?'

'Yes and no. Certain amount of threats, bad language, mainly from Precious as it happened.'

Miss Peterson shook her head.

'She must learn to control her temper. Who started it?'

'Not sure. Some chance remark from Denny, I think.'

'That young man never made a chance remark in his life.'

'No, indeed,' said Hopwood. 'The point was, it wasn't a remark about her. I think she can take that. It was a remark about you, Maureen.'

'About me?'

'Yes, not sure what. It referred to the fracas outside the gates the other afternoon. Whatever it was, Precious thought it was the last straw.'

'What about the other kids? Did they join in?'

Hopwood shook his head.

'Neutral mainly. Some don't like Denny. Some are afraid of him, particularly since he teamed up with Stebson.'

She nodded. 'I see. But Precious was ready to take on both of them?'

'No, funny thing was, it was Stebson who stopped it. Said something to Denny that cooled it.'

'Now why was that? I don't see Stebson as referee.'

'No more he is. My theory is that Stebson considers himself to be baron of 3H and he doesn't like people being nasty out of turn. Spoils his notion of peck order.'

'So, what have you done, Dan?'

'I've warned Denny that any more provocation and he'll be on the mat.'

'What did he say?'

'Nothing, just acted innocent.'

'So, what do you want me to do, then?'

'I don't know, Maureen. Can you give Precious an auntie talk? Tell her you can live with this, so must she.'

Miss Peterson suddenly looked sharply at Hopwood.

'Who says I can live with this kind of filth, Dan?'

He jerked back in surprise. Then recovered himself.

'Sorry, Maureen. I did get before myself then, didn't I?'

She smiled and put her hand on his arm.

'No offence, Dan, and I will talk to Precious.'

Chapter 21

Benny Green was waiting for Precious as she came tearing up the path to the gardens, out of breath.

'Hey, what's with you?'

'Sorry, Miss Peterson kept me.'

'Yeah?'

'Woman to woman talk, about something that happened earlier.'

They swung out on to the main road, keeping pace.

'I heard,' he said.

'What would you have done, Benny?'

He shrugged: 'Depends.'

'On what?'

'What you're being needled about, how often?'

'I don't know. I don't mind so much for myself. It just seemed with that dirt about Miss Peterson, he was getting at *us*, not personal like.'

He ran on in silence, breathing deeply, then turned and looked at the tall black girl.

'If it's not personal, then you have to watch when you get into a bundle.'

'Why?'

'Because you don't know how many you're fighting. And you need back-up on your own side.'

She nodded.

'There's just him, really like that.'

'What about Stebson?'

'Bad, but not bent, like Denny.'

'Maybe you should just wash him out. Let him be.'

'Right – if he'll leave me.'

'There's worse than Denny, and bigger.'

'Yeah. That's why I'm glad I'm not running on my own.'

Benny grinned.

'Come on,' he said. 'Let's do a quick lap of the park before the light goes. Give you ten yards.'

'You won't, you know.'

Chapter 22

After a bad start, the Easter holiday weather suddenly turned fine and warm. Tucker, feeling the blood surging in his veins, rang Pamela.

'Hi, kid.'

'Hello, Peter.'

'How about a spot of revision?'

'What, sit on a mouldy mattress in a damp flat on a day like this?'

'No, a better idea.'

'Are any of your ideas ever good, Jenkins?'

'If you are going to be like that, Cartwright, go ahead, fail your exams. But don't, repeat don't, come and wet my shoulder afterwards.'

'I'm listening, Peter.'

'Look, you get some sandwiches, a Thermos, whatever, and meet me at the bus stop at the top of Kettlewell, ten o'clock.'

'What are you bringing?'

'My expertise.'

'Ho ho. I mean book-wise. I mean we are revising.'

'You have a filthy mind, Cartwright.'

'I'll see you at ten o'clock, Peter.'

'The open-air centre? You have a nut loose, Peter.' Pamela stared at Tucker as the bus pulled away from the stop. She shook her head in despair. 'If it isn't a flat with dry rot, it's a cottage with woodworm.'

'Very useful to have somewhere if it rains.'

'Peter, it's not going to rain.'

'Yeah, but the grass is too wet to lounge about on,' said Tucker.

Towards noon they were walking down a narrow lane about

72

a mile from the centre. The sun was warm, the hedges full of blossom and the scent of flowers hung on the breeze. Pamela slipped her arm through Tucker's.

'Great, isn't it?' she said, leaning on him. He slipped his arm under her arm. They wrestled about a little, then settled for walking side by side.

At the foot of the slope, they turned aside, and hopped over a stream. Pamela dropped her shoe in the water and Tucker wet his jeans to the knee fishing it out.

'Let's eat,' she said at last.

'Yeah, indoors,' he answered. 'Too much fresh air gives you rheumatism.'

'O.K. Hey, how do we get in? Isn't it locked up?'

'Nah,' he said. 'The door wasn't properly hung, last time. It's just propped up.'

'What'll we sit on?'

'I expect there's a pile of straw or something left over.'

'Hope it's dry.'

'Cartwright, you're a worryguts.'

She stopped and pointed to the old building. 'Look, they made a worse job than you said. The door's hanging open.'

''Tis too. Still we can fix that.'

'You're so versatile, Peter.'

'You don't know how versatile I am.'

'I fear the worst,' she said.

They came up to the side of the building in silence. The door was indeed half open and the sunlight lit up the passageway beyond. As they crossed the threshold, Pamela's tights caught on a nail. She swore.

'Hey, I never thought you even knew that word,' said Tucker.

At the sound of their voices, there was a sudden flurry and rustling from the room beyond.

'What's that?' said Pamela.

'Rats,' said Tucker.

'Big ones.'

Tucker charged forward and flung open the inner door.

73

Sitting up foolishly on a pile of straw in the centre of the room were Susi and Alan.

'Let me guess,' said Tucker. 'You're revising, but you've forgotten your books.'

Chapter 23

Trisha Yates was heading through the Arndale when she ran into Cathy.

'Hi, Trish.'

''Lo, Cathy.'

'Where are you going?'

'. . . thought I'd go up to the library for some books I need.'

'Library's closed.'

'Oh, is it? I expect the reference is open, though.'

Trisha spoke too quickly and Cathy stared at her.

'You meeting somebody? You are, aren't you?'

'Well, if you know, there's no need to tell you.'

'Suit yourself.'

Trisha changed the subject rapidly.

'How did that gig go?'

Cathy made a face.

'Stood you up, did he?'

'No, he didn't.' Cathy was indignant. 'It was the others who let us down.'

'Well, that's better than nothing, I suppose. Saw your Gary's letter in the local rag. Bit strong, wasn't it? Was that Eddie Carver's doing?'

'Oh, no, Eddie Carver wanted our Gary to tone it down. Real smoothie he is.'

'Could have fooled me. He wasn't smooth with MacMahon at summer camp, was he?'

'No, he's very dodgy, Gary says.'

'I thought they were buddies.'

Cathy shook her head.

'No more. He's not talking to Carver these days. Neither's Dukeson.'

'Hey, what's going on?'

'Dunno Gary isn't saying. But I think Carver's up to something very funny.'

'Your kid had better stay clear of that.'

'Too right. Anyway, Trish. See you. Have fun with him.'

'Who says I'm . . .'

'Only kidding. See you.'

'See you.'

When she had shaken off Cathy, Trisha hurried to the café where she had met Jim before. She burst through the door and looked wildly round. Two old ladies looked up and glared at her. She could read their minds, 'Grange Hill typical'. But there was no Jim Hart.

She backed out and walked along to the shops, trying to interest herself in the displays, but without much success. That was the worst of getting to know somebody new and liking them. There was all this business, missing dates and wondering.

Someone slipped a hand under her arm. She jumped like a startled rabbit. It was Jim just behind her.

'You shouldn't do that to strange women. You get nicked for that,' she protested, grinning.

'Oh, I knew it was you – those glorious Vanderbilts.'

Ah. He hadn't made remarks like that before. She let him steer her back to the café and they entered arm in arm.

Now the old biddies would have something to chew over with their knitting.

Jim was in an inquisitive mood again with a stream of easy questions about school. Then they chatted about the school magazine. He was full of advice. Suddenly she asked:

'Jim, why are you so curious about our school?'

For a split second his eyes flickered, then he grinned.

'I write a bit, you know, school stories. It gives me colour. You know, school's changed a bit since my day.'

'Oh yeah, they don't use those slates and pencils any more, do they, granddad?'

He smiled: 'Do you mind, Trisha?'

'You're not a reporter, are you?'

'Well, I have done stuff for the local paper. Why?'

76

'Well, you could get something in about Grange Hill Something true for a change.'

'You're a funny girl, Trish.'

'So I'm told. Why?'

'One minute you're slagging the school and the Head and the restrictions and all. Next minute you get indignant when somebody else has a go.'

She raised her eyes to meet his.

'Well, it's different. One's in the family. One isn't.'

'Oh. And I'm not in the family, eh?'

'I didn't say that.'

He changed the subject quickly.

Trisha got home later than she had intended. Her mother and Carol were sitting in the kitchen.

She sensed there was something wrong when she came through the doorway.

'Is he nice?' said Carol, helpful as usual.

'Don't know what you mean.'

'You were seen.' Her mother never wasted words.

'So what?'

'He's older, a lot.'

'What the hell has that got to do with . . .?'

'Don't shout at me, Trisha. Just be careful. Older blokes are only after one thing . . .'

'Oh, Mum, don't be stupid. He's not after that . . .'

'Well don't sound so disappointed, Trish,' joked Carol.

Trisha glared at both of them and marched out, slamming the door.

Chapter 24

When Trisha reached school next day, she had an urgent message. There was a special meeting of the school magazine group in lunch break. When she reached the library, they were all there, Matthew, Christopher and McGuffy pacing the floor, waving his arms. What a mess he looks, she thought, just the opposite of Jim. The little Canadian girl, Belinda Zowkowski, was there as well.

McGuffy rubbed his hands.

'O.K., let's roll.'

They all sat down.

'First the bad news. The Head wants the magazine out much earlier this year. She's particularly keen on a good sale. It's very much a PR job for the school. Top and bottom is, the Head wants to see all the stuff this week.'

'She's going to read it all?'

'Every dot and comma.'

'No rude words in the quiz?'

McGuffy grinned. 'I hope we can sell this one to her, a mixture of straight stuff, comic stuff, some lively but provocative. It's a package.'

'This week?' said Trisha. 'I don't see how it can be done.'

Christopher spoke up. 'I think we can. It's mostly here already.' He tapped the pile of paper in front of him.

'But I thought you were short of stuff, decent stuff I mean.'

McGuffy raised his hand. 'I'll come in here and spare all the blushes.'

Now Belinda was blushing. Nice kid, thought Trisha. Bit up against it. But O.K. Trisha knew all about that.

'This is the good news,' went on McGuffy. 'Belinda has come up with a great piece of writing. A sort of diary. It's been edited a bit, but it's really fresh stuff, an outside look at Grange Hill from the inside, as it were.'

He grabbed the pile of paper and Belinda's face turned redder. 'Listen, this is great.'

He read:

'Advice to those about to grow up. Don't. At fourteen you get to pay full fares. At fourteen you get not to wear a seat belt legally and put your head through the windscreen. At fifteen they prosecute you for staying away from school. At sixteen you get to catch lung cancer, legally – and pregnant, legally. At seventeen they prosecute you for trying to get back in.'

He paused, Trisha grinned.

'Great, if the Head lets it by.'

'I think she will, with the other stuff. It's strong, but true. And,' he patted the bundle, 'there's more.'

'More diary?'

'Yes. But more more.'

'Like what?'

McGuffy leapt to his feet and paced up and down. He *was* different from Jim, thought Trisha.

'Matthew has come up with some computer stats which prove,' McGuffy paused, 'which prove that the authorities are selling Grange Hill short.'

'How?'

'They say that in ten years' time, there won't be enough kids to keep the school open. But Matthew's calculations, based on Government figures, show that there are other possibilities.

'Anyway, Stew has written it all up. And he's agreed that I'll do a little piece to introduce it, sort of "Grange Hill has a future".'

Trisha made a face.

'Wish I could believe it.'

McGuffy looked at her. 'Come on, Trish. At least this way we go down fighting.'

Chapter 25

McGuffy, full of excitement from the magazine meeting, went to the staffroom to grab a cup of coffee and walked into a row. As he entered, a group of teachers surrounded Golborne, who was pinning lists to the board.

Sutcliffe looked round.

'Hi. You look pleased with yourself.'

'Too right I am.' Before he could stop himself, he poured it all out. He knew he was being rash. He'd intended to keep the school magazine thing quiet, but his enthusiasm was too much for his discretion this time. Finally he held up Christopher's article and Matthew's print-outs and graphs.

'This proves there's no need to close Grange Hill or any other school in the area. No need for this cut-throat contest which is winding everyone up. No need for all this exam fever, no need for all this paper machine . . .' He stopped. Now he knew he'd gone too far.

Golborne turned from the board and looked over his spectacles.

'I'm all for enthusiasm, but can we set aside the authorities' predictions in favour of those of a third year enjoying himself with a computer?'

'I supervised Matthew's project. I checked his calculations and his conclusions,' said Miss Lexington. 'They're exemplary.'

Golborne smiled.

'My apologies.' He paused and adjusted his spectacles, looking round at his audience.

'If my mental arithmetic is right, Mr McGuffy, your conclusion is that we should keep the school going at all costs for over ten years in the hope it will fill up again . . .'

McGuffy swallowed. He hadn't expected an attack from

this quarter. He thought rapidly. Golborne smiled again. Miss Lexington intervened.

'Or you could say, wipe the school out because you're afraid you can't fill it, then have to build a new one at twice or three times the cost.'

Golborne smiled again. 'There are risks either way. My concern is that we face the financial situation as it is and try to make out of four schools three really efficient . . .'

'And overcrowded ones,' said Sutcliffe.

'Three excellent schools,' insisted Golborne. 'In industry in recent years, remarkable results have come from streamlining, rationalizing, cutting out fat   '

'Yeah,' stormed McGuffy, 'and now the fat's all on the dole.' The others stared at his furious face. He gestured wildly. 'Well, I didn't come into education to fart around like a time-and-motion man at British Leyland. I came to teach kids, give them and their parents something worthwhile.'

There was a silence, then Keating spoke quietly.

'I sympathize. But I wonder if the parents care at all whether this school survives? There is not much sign of interest in Grange Hill's future from that quarter, I fear.'

Baxter coughed.

'I think that's the bell, comrades.'

Chapter 26

McGuffy stayed on after school, trying to prepare his introduction to the school magazine article. But the words would not flow. The row in the staffroom had depressed him. He wrote one page, tore it up, wrote another. Soon the table was littered with screwed up sheets. He couldn't get it right. Doors opened and shut. Mr Thomson, the caretaker, and the cleaning ladies came and went. McGuffy worked on. Then he noticed the time. Good grief, it was a quarter past five.

He ran his tongue round his lips. They felt dry. There was one solution to that. He swept all the waste paper into the basket, stuffed the rest into his briefcase and wandered out. The school was deserted. Even the road outside was empty. After that little incident with Miss Peterson, the groups of school leavers had scattered. What could the school do to help them? he wondered. They couldn't just push kids out into the world and tell them to sink or swim. On the other hand, what could be done?

Ah well, he thought, one problem at a time. He absent-mindedly pushed back the swing doors of the pub on Broadwood and entered. It was nearly full, mainly blokes getting down a quick pint before going home. As he edged his way to the bar, he heard guffaws and loud coughing on his right. He ignored them. Then came a burst of applause.

'Brothers,' came a genial Irish voice. 'I give you the hope of the toiling masses of North London, Comrade McGuffy.'

His face red, McGuffy turned round. Grinning at him through the cigarette smoke were a round dozen of the men from the building site nearby.

The speaker was a powerfully built man, balding, with an open-neck shirt and bristling hair-covered chest.

'Oh, hello, Paddy,' he said, and sidled towards the bar. He couldn't sit with that mob. One round of whisky chasers and he'd be skint for the month.

'Come on, McGuffy, sit down,' Paddy didn't care if the whole pub heard. His blokes owned it. 'Come on, lad. Have one with us. I'm in the chair and the kitty's full. Won't cost you a penny.' Paddy was smart. The big man turned to his mates. 'It's a crying shame the way the working masses soak the middle classes. Now is the time to put it right.'

As Paddy pressed to the bar McGuffy sat and looked round. He knew some men by sight. The big black man with the stick hanging over the back of his chair was familiar.

'How's the revolution?' somebody asked at his elbow. McGuffy groaned to himself. Ever since he'd got into a drunken argument with the men from the site a month ago, they'd labelled him. He should learn to keep his mouth shut.

'How's the job going?' He tried to change the subject.

'Job? What job, squire?' said another. 'Finished. Topped off today. Next month we go and draw our oil money.'

'Oil money?'

'Dole, mate. That's where all the oil money's going, isn't it?'

Paddy was back and a pint was in front of McGuffy. As he drank deeply, he became aware that the black man was speaking.

'You teach at Grange Hill?'

He nodded.

'My kids go there.'

McGuffy looked blank. When would he be able to remember faces?

'Benny and Michael Green,' said the man.

'Oh yes, the footballer. Great kid.'

'Football, football. That's all he thinks of. Bit more attention to his studies is what he should pay.'

'Ah, come on, Sam,' boomed Paddy. 'All work and no play, y'know. It's not a bad school, as schools go.'

'True, and as schools go, it's going,' said one of the men.

'Do you think so, mate?' asked Sam Green. 'The word was it would be O.K. Councillor Doyle is the man who runs the

Education Committee. If he can't look after Grange Hill, who can?'

Paddy put down his glass.

'It grieves me to have to say it about a fellow countryman, but if I were you, Sam, I would not look for salvation from that quarter.'

'Why not?'

'Because the word is that now the elections are over and they're choosing the new committees, Councillor Doyle has his eye on fresh pastures.'

'Has he now?'

'So I am told. He's aiming to be chairman of the Finance Committee, which is as good as boss of the whole council. Then he has his eye on bigger things even, like Parliament, who knows?'

'How does that affect Grange Hill?'

'Well now, along the road, there's a lot of bargains made, horse trading. What if Doyle decides to butter up the people over Brookdale way? You could wake up one day and find "For Sale" notices on the school gate.'

He looked round. 'Mr McGuffy, your glass is empty.'

Chapter 27

Later that evening Sam Green and McGuffy stood outside the pub in the dusk.

'Which way are you going, Mr Green?'

'To the site. I have to check the gates.'

'Shall I walk along with you?'

'Don't bother. I have to go my own pace.' Sam Green brandished his stick.

Across the road, a lone tall figure trotted by. McGuffy smiled.

'Precious Matthews. Still training hard.'

Sam Green frowned. 'She's out late on her own. Our Benny usually runs with her.'

'I expect she knows what she's doing.'

'Hope so. Good night, Mr McGuffy.'

'Good night, Mr Green.'

McGuffy crossed the road and set an unsteady course for his flat, along Kettlewell Street. Without thinking where he was going, he picked his way through the side streets. The street lights had come on, but here and there bulbs were smashed, leaving patches of darkness. As he reached a corner, he saw Precious again, flitting by on the other side of the road. Several yards behind her two young fellows loped along in track suits. Black faces briefly caught the lamplight. He didn't recognize them.

He thought no more of it. Suddenly he thought about his article. He knew what to write. He saw a cartoon in his mind, a school gate with a notice hanging sideways:

'Grange Hill For Sale'

Chapter 28

Precious made her second circuit without meeting Benny.
Something must have happened. She felt cheated. The light
was nearly gone. She recalled what her mother had said
about sticking to daylight running, but made up her mind to
go round again. She felt in good form and she might meet
Benny this time.

It was then that the two blokes caught up with her. When
they were level with her, one on each side, she shot a quick
glance at them. They were black. No, they weren't. There
was something wrong about the faces. The eyes didn't move.
She put on pace and drew ahead. The tower block on
Broadwood loomed ahead. Her pursuers had caught up with
her again. One spoke:

'Dis chile am sure some mover.'

'Yey, man.'

They each placed a hand on her shoulder. She tried to
break free. They gripped tighter. They were running her
faster and faster. Now they had a hand under her arm and
with each step they lifted her from the ground.

'Let go, you . . .'

They ran her into a cul-de-sac by the chain mesh fence
around the building site. Ahead glowed the red lamps
around a pipe trench, a huge, dark gash across the road.

She dug in her heels and tried to halt. One of them slapped
her across the face. She got her hand free and struck back. It
wasn't flesh she touched, but a dry, smooth surface. They
were wearing masks.

They dragged her forward now, her feet scrabbled on the
edge of the trench and her back was bent over the plank
barrier.

She screamed. They let her scream. Once, twice.

'Here he comes,' said one.

Then they clapped a hand over her mouth and forced her backwards. The last she saw as she fell down, her head striking the jutting stones of the trench wall, was Benny Green, track-suited, charging down the road towards them. Then she landed deep down, and saw nothing more.

Humming to himself, Sam Green checked the last gate and set course for home. He was later than usual. Still, he wouldn't be coming home late from this job much longer. Nor would his mates. It was down the road for the lot of them.

Paddy had promised to keep an eye open for more work for Sam, if Paddy got a job himself. Still, no good thinking of that. Sufficient until the day was the evil thereof, so they said.

He paused in his slow progress at the neck of the cul-de-sac. Just check the lights on the pipe trench. He turned awkwardly on the rough surface, seeking a grip for his stick. Hello, that was wrong. There should be six lamps. Only four were showing. He tried to speed his pace. The plank barrier was broken. Vandals again. Should he leave it or should he fix those lamps? Some parking motorist might back in and that would be four thousand quid up somebody's shirt.

As he neared the edge of the trench he heard the first sounds of a voice calling for help. There was somebody in the trench!

'Hold on, I'm coming,' he shouted.

Chapter 29

McGuffy came into school next day in two minds. One of them was elated over the article *Grange Hill For Sale* he had finally written just after midnight. The other was coping with a hangover and feeling somewhat sick.

Within five minutes of reaching the staffroom he was shocked and sobered. White-faced he listened to Maureen Peterson and Geoff Baxter.

'I called in at the hospital,' said Maureen. 'Both as well as can be expected. Precious has slight concussion and a broken arm. Benny's collar bone is dislocated and he has multiple bruising.'

'It was Benny's father who found them?' asked Baxter.

'Yes, lying in a foot of water at the bottom of a pipe trench. It was due to be filled this week, before they start closing the site down.'

Eyeing McGuffy's white face, Miss Peterson went on: 'The baffling thing is who did it, and why?'

'Could be the same herberts who tried shoving you around outside school the other week.'

McGuffy interrupted. 'I – saw Precious running last night and there were two blokes following her. I didn't think . . . they seemed to me to be black.'

'Black?' said Baxter. 'That is weird . . .'

'Weirder still,' answered Miss Peterson, 'Precious says these characters who threw her down the hole had masks on.'

'Masks?' Baxter's voice rose.

'Yes, like black papier-mâché faces. And they were talking to her in sort of imitation – you know, minstrel style. Jeering.'

By now other teachers had come in and gathered round.

'That sounds like a set-up, something planned deliberately,' said Sutcliffe. 'That's diabolical. I'd like to get my hands on them.'

'We-ell, Graham, you have to remember the poor girl's concussed. She might have imagined it. I mean, why should they do it?'

'Could be one of these race gangs – harassment. Or somebody trying to get at the school . . .'

'Oh, come on.'

'You can say that. But what does it do to our soccer and sports chances?'

'Knocks a hole in them, I should say,' remarked Baxter gloomily.

McGuffy burst out: 'The worst is I could have stopped it. I saw them go by. But I was thinking about something else.'

'How could you know? We're all baffled.' Mr Keating, who had just come into the room, spoke: 'By the way, the Head wants to see you, quickly.'

'What about?'

'No idea. Doesn't look too good.'

It wasn't. As McGuffy entered the office, Mrs McClusky had the school magazine articles spread out over her desk. She looked at him coldly and started in without asking him to sit down.

'What were you thinking of, Mr McGuffy? I put you in charge of the pupils on this operation to bring a touch of maturity and wisdom, not to sensationalize the whole thing.'

McGuffy's headache suddenly bounced back at him. 'I don't quite follow.'

'Do you not? Well let me make it plain. Little Belinda's diary is a bit over the mark, but has a certain charm. She is after all only eleven. But this, which I understand you put on to my desk only this morning,' she waved McGuffy's hand-written sheets, 'totally lacks any such charm. You are more than twice as old as she, and about three times as irresponsible.'

'But I don't see . . .'

'Don't you? More's the pity. Can you not understand that

what we are trying to do is to avoid upset, to keep a low public profile for the school, improve its performance and make out an unbeatable case for staying open?'

'But Mrs McClusky, you're counting on the powers-that-be treating the school fairly. Suppose they're not. Suppose . . .'

The Head tapped on the desk with her pencil. 'Suppose you leave that to me. And suppose you now try and concentrate on what we are all supposed to be doing, making this school a success.'

'What about the magazine?'

'I've decided to cut our losses and cancel it. It's too late to repair the damage. We'll send out an extended issue of the school bulletin. Now, kindly find Trisha Yates and ask her to be responsible for collecting in all copies of every magazine item and delivering them to me.'

Later in the morning McGuffy found Trisha and told her. To his surprise, she simply stuck out her lip, muttered 'typical' and went away. Towards the end of the afternoon he saw her, arms full of papers, heading towards the office. She made a face at him as she passed, then grinned. Somehow he felt better.

But what neither McGuffy nor indeed any member of staff saw that day was Trisha, immediately school had ended, slipping into the library and feeding pages of all the articles into the photocopier.

Chapter 30

As school life moved slowly on towards the end of the summer term, things quietened down. There were no more incidents outside the gates, no more unpleasant letters in the Press. With the Boot Club disbanded and its sacred object, the old boot, hidden somewhere in Pogo's gear, the third year seemed to settle down and even do some school work.

Further up the age scale exam fever had struck and everyone had their heads down. Tucker had given up his attempts to organize private revision sessions with Pamela and squared up to his first papers with a mixture of confidence and desperation.

One day, he and Alan, who'd barely seen each other for several days, met briefly in the common room. Alan looked pale.

'You look even worse than usual, mate,' Tucker greeted him.

'Ta very much,' muttered Alan, sitting down and fiddling in his pockets.

'I'm gasping,' he said.

'What, for a fag? You're not going to, are you? I thought Hopwood and MacMahon had cured you. You getting withdrawal symptoms?'

'Well, this exam caper gets on your nerves. They reckon at Bristol University, people throw themselves off the Suspension Bridge during the exams and they have to keep the fuzz posted to stop them.'

'Great. You and Susi been on the straw lately?'

'What d'you mean?' Alan sat up looking offended.

'Well you know – revising?'

'Nah, you can't get any peace and quiet. I thought I had it made one time. Got a good idea. Get a one-stage ticket at Hayes Green, stay on the train till the terminus. Keep quiet till they start off again Right time of evening you can have an empty compartment for a couple of hours for fifty pence.'

'Not bad. Did it work?'

'Did it? A retired school teacher got on at the next stop, took the book off Susi and tested us all the way, then told us off for not knowing the answers.'

Tucker grinned. 'Hey, Benny's coming out next week. Pity that – I'll miss eating his grapes.'

'Dodgy business that. Who do you reckon did him over?'

'Brookies?'

'Not really. Benny says they looked black to him. But he barely saw them.'

'Precious reckons they had masks on.'

'Yeah, well, she got hit on the head, didn't she?'

'Funny all the same.'

'We should worry. We have our own problems . . .'

'True – like maths this afternoon.'

'You're joking.'

'I'm not. Look at your timetable.'

'Oh no.'

Chapter 31

Sergeant Harris was sitting late one evening over his paper work at the police station, when the rear door opened and Detective-Constable Charlie Taylor came through.

'What's this, Charlie, burning the midnight oil again? Won't do, you know. Super's been on to us about all the overtime.'

'And just how does he reckon we keep the patch covered?'

'Ah, yes, Charlie, but it's money, isn't it? Joe Public likes it on the cheap.'

'Don't talk to me about Joe Public.'

'Not if it upsets you, Charlie.' The sergeant looked at the gloomy face of the plain-clothes man. He closed his books, stuffed loose papers in a file and threw the lot into the open drawer at the side of his chair. Yawning, he stretched out his legs.

'Time for the cup that cheers *and* inebriates. Let me buy you one, Charlie, and you tell me all about it and we'll charge it up as an informer.'

They walked across the road and cut through the side streets to Broadwood. As they walked, Charlie talked.

'Had Paddy Riordan in today.'

'I should know him?'

'Big bloke off the site.'

'Oh yes? What did he want? Bit unusual, isn't it? We're not normally his first port of call.'

'No, he came in as backup to the black bloke, Sam Green, you know, handicapped feller, gatekeeper.'

They entered the pub and found one of the side rooms almost empty. Harris brought over the drinks.

'So, what did he want?'

'Wants to know why we haven't picked up the villians who

gave the coloured girl that working over and pushed Green's son in that pipe trench up the road.'

'What did you tell them?'

'Usual stuff Little to go on Pursuing certain lines of enquiry.'

'What did they say?'

'Not good enough.'

'In short, everyone performed as expected. So why the gloom and despondency?'

Charlie pulled on his drink: 'Strange as it may seem, Sarge, the case worries me.'

'Well, yes. Nasty. Nastier still when Joe Public leans on you. But look, Charlie, how long have you been at it now?'

'Seventeen years. Why?'

'Well, how many thousands of unsatisfied customers have you met in that time? How many cases of assault, GBH, general mayhem with no rhyme nor reason to them? In fact, that's what these herberts enjoy about it, doing it without rhyme or reason, then having a giggle at our expense.'

'True, Sarge, but this one's got a pattern to it.'

'Charlie, you've been watching Sweeney repeats again, haven't you? Of course it's got a pattern to it. Gangs of woodentops running round duffing up our Commonwealth relations.'

'I know. But this one's a bit different.' Charlie picked up the glasses and returned with another round. 'You know, I told you there's this group of Grange Hill graduates I've had my eye on.'

'Yes. So what have they done?'

'Nothing. That's it.'

'Charlie. You worry when they do, you worry when they don't. How is the average wrong-doer going to satisfy you?'

'Well, they don't seem to be doing anything. But some things have been done and we can't fit anybody to them.'

'Come on, Sherlock. Tell us the theory.'

'Right. A bloke, somebody with a touch of class, bit above your average Borstal bait, wants to start a new firm. Has ambitions above his station. Not content with crime, wants to make his mark. So he gets his team together, but holds them down. He's waiting, and planning to do something, something very naughty. Something that's going to have everybody saying, "we're impressed".'

'What particular naughtiness, Charlie? Be specific.'

'I don't know. If I did I'd go and have a word with him.'

'So you know who it is?'

'Do us a favour, Sarge. Of course I know who it is. That's the least of my problems.'

'Well?'

'Bloke called Carver, Eddie Carver. No form, but a lot of potential. A man we shall hear more of.'

'Have you told the inspector?'

'Yes.'

'And?'

'And he says – that is the Super says – I should start earning my daily bread for a change. I've been advised to devote my attention to the grown-ups – like the boys on Broadwood.'

'Mr Riordan's company?'

'That's it. It seems they've been having meetings with Grange Hill teachers.'

'Supping Guinness more like.'

'Super says, given the situation, they should be watched.'

'So, what'll you do?'

'Keep my eye on both.'

'Good thinking. But watch it, Charles. Superintendent Oakley can be less than charming. You don't want to wind up riding your bike again. Not at your age.'

Chapter 32

Just in the last week of the exams, the local paper started running its exclusive series on Grange Hill. *The Inside Story* was the headline, and so it was. In two articles the un-named writer – A Special Correspondent – went through the card – school uniform aggro, common room aggro, smoking, drinking, pregnant sixth-formers. The Boot Club got most of an article to itself.

And to crown it all came a special editorial headed *A Bad Press*, which said, among other things:

'School heads in comprehensive schools often lament that the local Press is unfair to them, that they have a bad Press. The truth, they say, is much more wholesome and encouraging.

'Our special series shows that we have been somewhat mealy-mouthed. In fact we haven't matched up to the school at all. But now at last we feel that we, and the public, have caught up with reality.

'It is no secret that the local authorities are now debating what to do with our four local secondary schools. The hard facts of life seem to suggest one of them should go.

'Perhaps if that one were to be Grange Hill, it might be an act of mercy, putting staff, pupils and above all parents, out of their misery.'

Trisha had the first article waved under her nose at breakfast time by her mother. She read it through with a sinking feeling in her stomach. That day at school she made a complete mess of her exam paper and wondered at the end how she'd found the strength even to sit down and answer the questions.

She avoided the group that gathered in the common room arguing over the article, but she heard people saying: 'They must have got that stuff from somebody in the school.' She,

Trisha, knew 'they' had got it from somebody in the school. She knew who 'they' had got it from, and she knew who 'they' were, or rather who *he* was. She had been hung out – all those great, heart-warming, flattering chat-ups in the library and the caff, all those throw-away remarks about her dress sense and style, her spirit, etc. etc. She had been a stupid little cow and that was just the start of it.

But the full extent of the treachery only came with the second article – even more lurid than the first. And even that was not the worst of it. The worst was that the crafty sod had not used any of that stuff she had given him from the school magazine, all those statistics, the arguments *against* closing the school. She had thought she was doing the smart thing, photocopying that stuff and slipping it to Jeremy bleeding Hart. He had taken everything she had told him, the good and the bad, and had used just what *he* wanted.

One day as she slouched along the school corridor, she overheard somebody say: 'What's up with Yates? She looks sicker than a cat on a grass diet.'

'Been stood up, I bet.' Stood up? They didn't know the quarter of it!

But if Trisha was sick, someone else was sicker. Mrs McClusky summoned the staff to a special session and spread the articles out over her desk. She was livid.

'We have to find out who gave them all this.'

As usual, Mr Keating tried to pour oil on the troubled waters.

'I don't think a witch hunt would do any good. And anyway, the horse has gone. No good shutting the stable door now.'

Mr Sutcliffe spoke up. 'Well, I think this is all gossip and what is more, selected gossip. It's a hatchet job. Someone wants Grange Hill closed down and this is just to soften up public opinion. So much for our low profile. So much for the eyes down, look-in approach.'

'I'm afraid I think there is more substance to it than that.' Golborne raised a shining shirt cuff and adjusted his spectacles. 'I'm afraid this is more or less the end product of an approach to school discipline which, while based on the best of intentions, has been somewhat too relaxed.'

'I'm afraid I tend to agree,' said Terri Mooney.

'Just a minute,' said Baxter, visibly heating up. 'Let's not sell the school short, whatever other people do.' He raised his hand and counted off on his fingers. 'Despite the injuries to Benny Green and Precious Matthews, we drew in the soccer final – Brookdale only went ahead on aggregate. And we came second in the athletics – very creditable.

'And,' he paused and looked round, 'we beat Brookdale at cricket, only by a single run, it's true.'

Hopwood smiled: 'Yes, if Patterson hadn't fallen over and stopped their last boundary, we'd have lost.'

'A win's a win,' snorted Baxter.

'I agree,' said Keating. 'The pupils have tried hard, and all the staff have tried hard, though we've been hard pressed to cover all classes during illness. And I personally think the exam results will be among our best in recent years.'

'I agree,' said Miss Peterson. 'By next term who will remember this rubbish?' She indicated the local paper. 'Who knows, by then we may have something to celebrate.'

Chapter 33

But someone was already celebrating. That night in the Steak House up at the Arndale, who should be gathered round a plate of medium rare and french fries and a bottle of Château Plonk but the Famous Four. Tucker, against advice from Doctor Humphreys, had indulged in a scotch on the rocks before sitting down at table and he was in a particularly celebratory mood. He sat with his glass held nonchalantly in his left hand, while his right arm was around Pamela's shoulders.

'Peter,' she said, 'togetherness is all right, but isn't this a bit public?'

Tucker looked round the restaurant. The sudden twist of his head made the tables and chairs shift somewhat in his vision, and he paused a while to let everything settle down.

'Public? What public? Just a lot of peasants getting above themselves. Hey, no, wait. Who's that in the far corner, Alan?'

'Which?' Alan, sitting alongside Susi, began to turn.

'Don't look now, but your old sparring partner is there, on his jack.'

Alan stopped turning. 'Which sparring partner?'

'Remember, under the greenwood tree, up the tower block stairs.'

Susi put her hand to her mouth: 'Not Eddie Carver?'

'The same.'

'Oh, stop it, Peter,' said Pamela, 'this is supposed to be a celebration. The exams are over.'

'We've all failed,' said Tucker.

'. . . we've all passed,' insisted Pamela, 'and we're enjoying ourselves. Some,' she said with a sideways look, 'more than others.'

Tucker rose, with the help of the chair back.

'If my company is disagreeable to you, madame,' he said in a loud voice, causing heads to turn at other tables, 'I will call the manager and have myself thrown out.'

'Oh box it, Tucker,' said Alan, and rising he forced Tucker back into his place.

Tucker resumed his careful study of the restaurant.

'Now there's someone I recognize. That bloke with a beard near the door. On the other side.'

Susi looked, then nodded. 'You know who that is?'

'No, do you?'

'Not really, but I tell you who does. Trish Yates.'

'You're joking.'

She shook her head. 'I'm not. That's the bloke she's been seen with.'

'Hey, he's old enough to be her dad. Probably married as well.'

'Peter. Don't talk rubbish. That man's no more than thirty, and rather dishy, I'd say.'

'You have no taste, young woman,' said Tucker, focusing on Pam.

'You can say that again,' put in Alan, 'look who she's out with.'

'What shall we have for sweet?' said Susi hastily.

Fifteen minutes later when coffee had been served and Tucker had been persuaded not to call for a balloon glass of Rémy Martin, Susi suddenly gasped and grabbed Alan's arm.

'Look at that!' Now all turned and stared at the door. Trisha Yates had entered and was heading for the table where the bearded man was sitting.

'Hm. Look at that. Pongo's geared up.'

'Sh, Peter, she'll hear you.'

But Trisha was listening to no one. She bore down on the table where the man sat, while her four school mates watched in fascination. The man rose.

'Hello, Trish,' he said quietly. 'I thought you might not turn up.'

100

Trisha spoke calmly, but her voice, pitched high, carried through the room. All the other tables suddenly went quiet.

'I wouldn't have missed this for anything.'

He sat down. 'Well, shall we eat?'

She paused.

'Well, since you ask, no. I don't usually eat with rats. In fact I don't think they should be in here at all. They belong round the dustbin. I ought to tell the health – authorities.'

Her voice wavered. He looked round in alarm. 'Trish, shouldn't . . .'

'You bastard,' she shouted, and rushed out.

Pamela leapt to her feet.

'I'm going after her,' she said and hurried across the restaurant.

Shrugging, Tucker got to his feet, and the other three made their way after Pam. As they rose, the waiter hastened to cut off their retreat.

'Oh no,' said Susi, 'the bill.'

'Tell him to put it on – my account,' said Tucker. Behind him Alan groaned.

When the three had left, Eddie Carver moved over to Hart's table and stood at his side.

'Can I have a quick word with you?' he said.

Hart looked up questioningly. Carver went on:

'I think I have something that might interest you'

'Who might you be?'

'Never mind that. Do you want to hear it?'

Hart shrugged: 'Why not?'

Chapter 34

The holidays were over, and the exam results were through. On the whole, they were good. Tucker had one subject to retake. Trisha, in spite of her upset during the exams, had managed to get through in all subjects. Everyone came back to school quietly, as if waiting for something to happen.

They did not have long to wait.

Towards the end of the first week, Mr Keating came into the Head's office. She sat with a letter in her hand.

'Mrs McClusky,' said Keating, 'I wonder if you would mind very much getting on to the Divisional Office and twisting their arms a bit. They say we can't have any supply teachers.'

She did not answer. He went on:

'We have to have them. We are seven teachers short today and the staff quite frankly do not feel inclined to put themselves out any more taking classes for absent friends. We had an unspoken agreement last year that until the exams everyone would bend the rules and tide us over. Now it won't work. So could you please . . .?'

Mrs McClusky looked up, her face pale, lips pressed together.

'Mr Keating, I don't think I want to speak to the Divisional Officer. I don't think I want to speak to Councillor Doyle, nor the Lord Mayor. If the Pope himself offered me an audience this morning, I'd turn him down. If I speak to anyone in authority today I shall make an exhibition of myself.'

'What on earth?'

She held out the letter.

'It's from the Education Officer. We are being closed down. Whether they just let us waste away or take the axe to us depends on further discussion. But they are closing us down.'

'But, I thought Councillor Doyle would . . .'

'Councillor Doyle is no longer chairman of Education. He has flown to a higher perch. He is bravely speaking up for us in various meetings, but says he can do no more.'

She laid down the letter.

'I feel so angry I could spit blood. I'm sorry, that doesn't help your problem. I expect I'll find strength to speak to the office about sending us someone. But in the meantime, can you cope somehow?'

Keating looked at her carefully.

'I'll do my best, Head.' He hesitated. 'Can I call on *anyone* – all the Senior Staff?'

'Anyone, Mr Keating. I'll lend a hand myself this afternoon, but this morning I have other fish to fry.'

Keating nodded and went out. Left to herself, the Head looked again at the letter, then put it down. She breathed deeply once or twice, then bending down she pulled from a drawer a bulky file. From it she extracted some papers, among them Matthew's computer calculations and McGuffy's handwritten article.

She was deep in her study of them when Mr Golborne entered the office, without knocking. She looked up at him in surprise.

'Mr Golborne?'

'Er, Head. I've just been informed by Mr Keating that I am to take Class 4H for two periods.'

'Well, we are very short-handed, Mr Golborne.'

'But,' he said agitatedly, 'I thought there was an understanding I should concentrate on . . .'

'On organization, Mr Golborne. That's quite true. But today it's all hands to the pump. Now if you'll excuse me, I've urgent matters to attend to.'

She looked up as Golborne closed the door behind him and called:

'4H are a very interesting bunch, you know.'

Chapter 35

4H, left on their own for ten minutes, were brewing up very nicely when the signal came from the lookout near the door.

'Guess who?'

'Sooty?'

'Nah.'

'Mooney?'

'Get off.'

'Keating?'

'Never.'

'The Boss?'

'No. It's your friend, my friend, everybody's friend – Goldenballs.'

Mr Golborne entered the room to a storm of cheering. He hesitated. His glasses seemed to have misted over. He removed them and the massed ranks of pupils suddenly became fuzzy and distant. He hastily polished the glass and replaced the spectacles. He could not believe it.

'You, the ginger-headed boy. What is that you have on your desk?'

'This, sir?' came the innocent reply. 'It's a boot, sir.'

'A boot?'

'Yes, sir, an old boot.'

Half-way through the period Miss Mooney had to leave her lab to fetch something from the staffroom. Leaving her charges with the demonstrator she made her way swiftly down the corridor. She heard 4H from some distance. She did not believe it. Wembley on Cup Day was a mere whisper to this. She increased her pace, then broke into a run. Short staffing was one thing, but leaving 4H on their own was a major crime. As she reached the door and plucked it open, there was pandemonium. A blizzard of paper pellets and clips filled the air, a couple of minor fights had broken out and at the back, smiling complacently and stroking an old boot which perched on his desk, sat Pogo Patterson.

Miss Mooney stormed in.

'4H!' she yelled.

She took them by surprise. Silence fell. The brawlers let go of each other's hair and ties, the volleys of projectiles lessened and stopped. The old boot had vanished from Patterson's desk like magic, to be replaced by a book in which he was suddenly and deeply interested. It was upside down.

'4H,' she said more calmly, 'you are disgusting. Stop sniggering. You know the school is short of teachers. You know the staff is doing its best. But you lot, the moment you are left to your own devices, you behave like hooligans. I shall discuss with Mr Hopwood what we shall do, but if I have my way, it'll be detention from now until Christmas.'

Suddenly she turned and stared at the teacher's table.

'And that boy hiding behind there, come out,' she commanded.

From behind the table came a sorry figure, suit chalk-stained, face pale, and clutching his steel-rimmed spectacles. Miss Mooney stared.

'Oh, I beg your pardon, Mr Golborne. I didn't know you were in charge.'

Chapter 36

That week a number of meetings took place. Some were accidental and some weren't.

Christopher Stewart stopped Trisha Yates on her way to the common room.

'Have you heard?'

'Don't want to.'

'We're doing the school magazine again.'

'You're out of your box.'

'No, we're using all the gear we had before. The Head's sending a copy out to every parent.'

'I'll believe it when it happens.'

'It's happened.'

Councillor Doyle met the chairman of the education committee at the Town Hall. The chairman looked annoyed to say the least.

'Have you seen this?' He waved a sheet of paper. 'A letter from all the staff at Grange Hill. It's offensive to say the least.'

Doyle shrugged: 'You'll be getting another from the governors – just as bad.'

The chairman confronted Doyle furiously. 'Look, you promised me I'd have a free hand over Grange Hill. Now you're . . .'

'No, I'm not,' protested Doyle. 'They insisted. I had to go along with them.'

The chairman prodded Councillor Doyle in the chest with his finger. 'One of these days you'll go along with someone a bit too far.'

Sam Green picked his way slowly through the crowd of

regulars in the pub on Broadwood to the table where Paddy Riordan sat with his mates. He sank down into a chair and looked at them.

'Why so depressed, gentlemen?'

'Not depressed, just reflective,' answered Paddy.

'Oh yes.'

'We've just had young McGuffy in here.'

'Ah, forecasting world revolution, eh?'

'A bit more direct and to the point. To be honest, Sam, he was slagging us all out — as parents, as citizens and as members of the Great Unwashed.'

'Now why should he do that?'

'He wanted to know what we were going to do about Grange Hill.'

Sam sat upright.

'That's a good point. What *are* we?'

The parents' meeting in the school hall was not at all accidental. And to be honest it wasn't very well-behaved either. At one point it made even 4H sound like a bunch of monks on a silence kick. At last Mr Humphreys, who was in the chair, got to his feet.

'Let's have a bit of order, please. I think you have all said what you think about the plan to close Grange Hill. I think, too, that I must ask all further speakers not to spend valuable time saying what they think of the Government, what they think of the Council or what they think of our Chairman of Governors, Councillor Doyle. They must have a fair crack of the whip.'

'Yes,' shouted someone from the hall, 'and I'll give it to them.'

Mr Humphreys raised his hand. 'That'll do now, Mr Green.'

He turned to the platform.

'Having said all that, there are one or two remarks I'd like to make. Many of us are disturbed. It seemed that Grange Hill was to have a fair chance to compete with other schools, show what it was made of. Now I think, and so do others, that in spite of various gutter stories in the Press, Grange Hill, staff and pupils, have done their best.'

He raised his hand to quell the applause.

But now it seems it didn't matter what they did, the school is going down the tube. It's not good enough.

'Now,' he turned to the audience, 'we're running short of time. We can take a few more speakers. Only let's have some thoughts on what we shall do.'

Mrs Green rose at the back of the hall and began to speak even before Mr Humphreys called her.

'I, for one, happen to disagree with Mr Humphreys. I don't think they should close any school, not while there's a need for it. And goodness knows, our children need schools.'

She paused.

'All these facts and figures Mrs McClusky sent to us. I don't entirely understand them, but I understand enough to know that if the council closes Grange Hill down, it will be making one big mistake.'

She looked up at the platform. 'I won't say what I think about Mr Doyle. But I will say this to him. This is *our* school. We send *our* children here. We raise money for it, we organize jumble sales for it, we bake cakes and we make jam for it. We even eat beans for it. So you can't take it away from us.'

'But Mrs Green, what do you want us to do?' asked Humphreys.

'I'll tell you what I want us to do, Mr Humphreys. I'll tell you something. It's the squeaky wheel that gets the oil.'

'Hear, hear,' yelled someone.

'I want us to make such a noise, they won't forget it. And when they come to us like they do every year or so and ask very nicely for us to vote them in again, we shall tell them – no, you're surplus to requirements, we don't need you, we can't afford you, we're closing you down . . . We . . .'

Whatever else Mrs Green said was never heard because the whole hall began to cheer and stamp their feet.

Chapter 37

Dear Diary Person,

I regret to say Dad and I have had words. He wanted me to leave Grange Hill and go elsewhere. Grange Hill is not a nice school in his eyes.

But he is so wrong. Grange Hill is not *nice*, but it is exciting. There is never a dull moment.

I've told you before of the famous Mr Golborne. I mustn use his nickname, because these days this Diary is liable to be published, so we must be more mature.

Anyway, the famous Golborne, having been destroyed, but utterly destroyed, by the Boot Club, is thinking of quitting Grange Hill and going to the Bahamas or wherever.

Funny thing is he bugged the staff even more than he did us kids. But they couldn't get rid of him. We did though.

What next? Another reason why Dad wanted me to leave Grange Hill is because they are about to close it down, so they say.

But that is not the end of the tale. No way. This morning coming to school along Broadwood Road, what did we see hanging from the new tower block but a stupendous banner, which the men there had put up. It said:

GIVE GRANGE HILL A CHANCE

Fairer than that you cannot say. What's more, around school today, people are singing a song made up by a girl in Upper School called Cathy. And it goes: 'Give Grange Hill a Chance, Mr Council Man, Give Grange Hill a Chance.' Very catchy tune.

Next week the whole school is turning out for a protest march. So stay with us. There'll be more.

Belinda

Chapter 38

Either the excitement of the day had been too much or the pie bought at the chippy had been somewhat off. The fact was the President of the Boot Club was out of sorts all afternoon. He tried once to get out of class, but Dan Hopwood was in no mood to take any more malarkey from Douglas Patterson.

So by the time school ended Pogo was about to explode three ways. Instead of heading for the school gate he rushed across the yard to the lavs. Once inside he had to think quickly. There were five places to choose from, in order of inconvenience.

Two had no light in them because the bulbs had been nicked. One had no toilet-roll holder and so no paper, one had no lock and one had no seat. Pogo did not have much time. He chose the one furthest from the door so he'd be undisturbed and rushed in. He saw to his relief that it had a lock and clicked it shut. He could tell there was a toilet holder, though there was no light. Did it have a seat? He sat down. No, it hadn't. He bounced up again, then gritted his teeth and sat down again. Five minutes later he felt civilized again and was about to get up when he stopped. He heard footsteps outside, then murmuring voices. Then the click of a lighter and the smell of smoke drifted through to him. He'd better sit tight. If this was a bunch of fifth years having a crafty drag, he'd be welcome as flowers in May.

Next he heard voices. He sat even tighter now. He didn t dare move. First Denny Rees:

'Listen, do you want in or not?'

Then Gripper Stebson:

'What's in it?'

'A ten.'

'Each?'

'No, between us.'

'Screw that.'

'Hey listen, I daren't ask Eddie for more. He'll kill me if he knows I've talked.'

'That's your funeral. What d'you want me in for?'

'Pass the bubble if anyone shows, while I get through the window.'

'What d'you do then?'

'Put this little packet in the broom cupboard and take off.'

'What packet?'

'Dunno. Eddie didn't say. I've got an idea.'

'So have I. I think you're off your runners and so's he. You'll get lumbered.'

'Nah. All I have to do is get through the window, leave it and get out. I'm allowed twenty minutes. It's dead easy.'

'Why can't Carver do his own job?'

'No, he says he wants a littler bloke to get in that way, like they did in Oliver Twist.'

'Jesus! Did he say that? Listen, you woodentop, d'you know what happened to the geezer in Oliver Twist, when he got through the window?'

'No.'

'He got nicked, didn't he? Forget it, Reesy.'

'Listen, mate. It'll be a doddle. We can't get nicked. We go in there when there's nobody in except the caretaker. Nobody there – see.'

'Forget it.'

'You mean you haven't got the bottle, Stebson.'

'Listen, you.' There was a scuffle, a cry of pain, then 'Don't let me hear you say that again – ever.'

And the voices died away.

Five minutes later, Pogo, still shaking, caught up with Matthew Cartwright on his way out of school. Matthew listened to him, amazed.

'Hey, let's go and tell Hopwood.'

111

Pogo shrank. 'No, if Gripper finds out, I'll get my legs busted this time, I know it.'

Matthew nodded. 'Tell you what, I'll have a word with our kid.'

Chapter 39

In the flat at the top of the tower block, looking down on Grange Hill, Pam and Tucker sat on camp stools by the window. Tucker held binoculars and from time to time scanned the school now in darkness, though its outlines showed up in the street lights.

'Peter, it's nearly midnight. Do you think we need to stay any longer?'

'Yeah. Now might be the time when they do it. Look, kid, you have a sleep. I'll wake you up a bit later.'

'You're only half awake yourself, Peter. I mean how long can we keep it up? This is the second night we've been here, Alan and Susi have done two nights. And nothing's happened.'

'I know, but I still feel something's going to.'

'Why are you so sure?'

'Cause Carver does not offer tens to little herberts like Denny Rees to pop packets through school windows for nothing. It smells. That's why Gripper kept out of it. He knows when a job's bent or not.'

'Do you really think it's a fire bomb, Peter?'

'Could be. Benson tried to set fire to the school, didn't he?'

'Not seriously.'

'Yeah, but Carver's a serious bloke, isn't he? Even if he is bent, he's not a brick-head, is he? He thinks. He's after something.'

'Yes, well maybe we should tell the police or something?'

Tucker looked at Pamela a moment.

'I think we've got to nick them and no messing. Because if we don't and Carver and Benson get any idea of who blew the whistle, it'll be intensive care for one or two people we know.'

'Another problem, Peter. I'm running out of excuses at

home. My parents are very broad-minded. Sometimes I wish they weren't so broad-minded. They suspect I'm having it away with my boy-friend, only they don't like to ask me in case I am.'

'Well, we can soon put 'em out of their misery, can't we. said Tucker.

Pamela glared. 'No *thank* you, Peter.'

Tucker picked up the binoculars and studied the school building again, concentrating on the side where the rooms were that housed old Tom Tom's cleaning gear. There was nothing there. Once earlier on he'd thought he spotted something, but it was only a lovesick cat. He laid the binoculars aside. He was dozing off.

Suddenly he was wide awake. He turned to Pam.

'Hey, wake up!'

She answered sleepily. 'What is it, Tucker? I was well away.'

'Get up, we're going home.'

'Why? It's only half past eleven.'

'I know. There's no point staying. I've just realized. We've been wasting our time.'

'How d'you mean?'

'Denny Rees said he'd go in when nobody was there, didn't he?'

'Yes.'

'And we thought it meant at night. But it doesn't. It means when we're all out on the demo. That's what Carver's after. While Grange Hill pupils are on the streets, the school goes up in smoke. That's it!'

'That means . . .'

'It means tomorrow.'

Chapter 40

The day of the demo there was glorious autumn sunshine, blue skies and a warm breeze. School finished at lunch time and by half past two, Grange Hill staff and pupils began to assemble outside the gates. Gradually, as more classes lined up, the road outside the school filled up, and women began to come from the houses and flats around to line the pavements.

The school band were trying out Cathy's song. At first they were ragged and the third years fell about laughing at them, but before long they had it right and blasted out with the tune. People began to join in:

'I went to school, I worked and I played,
Did all I could to get a good grade,
For all I tried, I might as well have stayed
    At home.
Grange Hill, Grange Hill,
They're taking you away,
Grange Hill, Grange Hill,
What more can I say?
Councilman, Mr Councilman,
Just give Grange Hill a chance,
A little chance,
Just give Grange Hill a chance.'

Marshalled by Bullet Baxter in his track suit, whistle round his neck and loud-hailer in his hand, the line-up began to take shape.

In front came the sports teams, Benny Green leading the soccer eleven. Precious Matthews, completely recovered and lively as ever, led the athletics team.

Then came the years, youngest first. The Head had relaxed the uniform rule for the day, and the result was that almost everyone had turned up in Grange Hill blazer and tie.

In the middle the Drama Department had mounted a tableau on the back of a truck loaned, and driven, by Alan's dad. It showed a knight in armour, brilliantly played by Graham Sutcliffe, destroying a dragon. Rumour had it that at first the dragon's head had been fitted with a mask strongly resembling Councillor Doyle, but at the last minute the Head had spotted it and had it removed.

At last all was in order and the Head and Mr Keating walked slowly down the parade, checking up on each contingent.

'One thousand people take up an awful lot of room, Head,' remarked Keating cautiously.

'All the better,' she replied, 'then they can't miss us.'

The Upper School brought up the rear behind an enormous banner which read: 'Will the real Grange Hill Stand Up?'

'All right, Maureen?' asked Mrs McClusky.

'All present and correct, except for five people.'

'Oh, who are they?'

'Jenkins, Cartwright, Yates, MacMahon and Humphreys.'

'I'm surprised, I'd have thought they would have made certain they were here.'

'They certainly helped get it all ready, Head. But right at the last moment, they disappeared.'

'I suppose that is typical, of Jenkins at least.'

The Head turned to Baxter.

'I think we are ready, Mr Baxter.'

'Ready when you are, Mrs McClusky.'

As they moved up to the head of the procession, Mr Keating appeared at Mrs McClusky's side.

'You do realize that by the time we get to the High Street, it'll be near rush hour conditions. It could cause a snarl-up.'

The Head looked thoughtfully at Mr Keating.

'Do you know, I believe it will.'

Chapter 41

No sooner had the demo wound its noisy way out of the road alongside the school, when a small, grey van drew up at the school gates. Six people struggled out of the back, and Eddie Carver got out from the seat by the driver. He turned and said, 'Just park in that side street and wait. Don't drop off, we may need you.'

From under their coats the six began to unfold large sheets of paper. Spread out, these were rough posters done in black paint.

'All right, spread out across the gate. Hold 'em so they can get the message. And try to look as if you mean it.'

'I feel stupid, Eddie,' said Benson, as he held his poster in front of his jacket.

'There's no answer to that,' replied Carver levelly. 'Listen, mate, just relax. In half an hour it'll be over and we'll be away. The job'll be done.'

'Yeah, and maybe we'll be done, as well.'

'Knock it off. Nobody is going to be able to fit us up for this, but nobody.'

'But we'll be right here when it goes up,' said one lad.

'Are you chickening out, mate?'

'Nah. But they can work it out, can't they? We'll be here in front of the bleeding cameras. Everybody'll see we're here!'

'If the television geezers come,' said another.

'I don't know why I bother,' said Carver. 'Listen, first of all the cameras *are* coming. Hart's seeing to that. It's worth it to him.'

'How do we know?'

'Work it out. He did that stuff on Grange Hill in the local rag, didn't he? So it gets picked up in the national Press, doesn't it? And the television gets on to it. So that's good for Hart, isn't it? And it's good for us. What more d'you want?'

'How d'you know the camera crew won't stay down at the High Road? That's where the police are, that's where the action'll be.'

'Action, what action? Lot of kids and teachers going for a walk? Listen, if you were a bloke on the television and you had a choice between that, and being on the spot when the school goes off, which would you do?'

'Yeah, but how do they know that's going to happen?'

'They don't. D'you think I'm a brick-head? All they know is something very special's going to happen. And we make sure they're on the spot, not after it happens like in Belfast but before it happens. It's a scoop – get it? They get awards for this kind of stuff – and Hart gets his slice. So he's doing what we tell him.'

'I still say they can fit us up for this job if we're here,' said Benson.

'Look, I'll spell it out for you again,' said Carver. 'If the school goes up and you, matey, tell the filth that you were the other side of town, you're going to get nicked. If it goes up and you are right out here, exercising your democratic rights to protest about what's going on, you can't be matched up for doing it. Get it?'

Benson was silent. One of the lads shouted, 'Here they are.'

Two cars drew up. Hart jumped out of the first and cameramen began to struggle out of the second with their gear.

Hart walked up to Carver.

'Well, we're here. Up to you now.'

'Don't worry. It's all laid on. And remember. You got an anonymous tip-off.'

Hart smiled with just a touch of contempt.

'Don't worry. I never reveal my sources.'

'Too right you don't, mate,' said Carver and looked Hart in the eye.

Hart's gaze dropped. The cameramen were coming towards them.

'So?'

'Any minute now,' said Carver.

'It'd better be. That demo could be coming back.'

Carver looked at his watch.

'No, mate. They'll be just at the High Street now, and do you know what? The police'll hold 'em up there for us and let the traffic through. How convenient.'

Hart looked away.

Chapter 42

PC Benson was at the main intersection in the High Road as the head of the demo approached. Sergeant Harris was a little way down the road. He strolled towards the constable

'Feeling the heat, Alf?'

Benson lifted his helmet and wiped his forehead.

'Could do with a cup of tea, Sarge.'

'When this lot's over, I'll buy you something a little stronger, Alf. Now just between you and me, Superintendent Oakley and the heavy mob are lying back across the way there, and I for one do not want them under our feet. I've had a word with that bloke Baxter, who's marshalling the whole issue. He's given me his oath that if we just hold the traffic up for five or six minutes, he'll get 'em over at the double.'

'Five or six minutes is a long time, at rush hour, Sarge.'

'I know, Alf, but if we keep these kids hanging about, or if we split the parade up in sections and let the traffic through piecemeal, it's going to get very hairy. Then we will have the heavy mob in.'

The constable nodded.

Behind them came the ear-splitting sound of the school band opening up, and the High Road with its massed traffic was suddenly filled with the strains.

'Grange Hill, Grange Hill,
They're taking you away,
Grange Hill, Grange Hill,
What more can I say?'

'Right, Alf. You to the right,' Harris signalled to PC Benson. 'I to the left, and may the best man win.'

'Oh no,' thought the constable, as he raised his gloved arm and brought the traffic on his side of the intersection to a halt, and the school band marched into the empty space.

With a screech of brakes, a blue car, light winking, swung

out of a side street and into the space alongside the marchers

'Sergeant!' Superintendent Oakley thrust his head from the car rear window.

'Sir.'

'What are you up to, man? Don't stop the traffic.'

'Quicker this way, sir.'

'Sergeant. I want this demonstration held up and the traffic let through.'

Harris glanced at Benson across the road, then motioned to the school marchers to halt.

But at that moment, from either side of the main road with a tremendous roar and grinding of gears, two huge yellow dumper trucks laden with spoil from the Broadwood building site drove together, meeting head-on with a great clang.

Superintendent Oakley leapt out of the car with a ripe oath.

Striding across to the trucks, which now effectively sealed off the main road on the right-hand side, he yelled, 'What are you maniacs playing at?'

From the cab of the nearest truck a large red face looked down.

'A slight miscalculation, Officer. Shall we back out?'

'Get these bloody machines out of here.' The superintendent was now very near losing control.

Both drivers started their engines at once, the trucks jerked, heaved, came together with a crash and the motors died.

Paddy looked down again from the truck.

'I'm sorry to have to tell you, sir, but it seems to have stalled.'

Superintendent Oakley kept his feet on the ground with an effort.

'Damn it, man! Use the distributor leads, can't you?'

'The what, sir? I'm not used to this vehicle, sir, I'm just driving it for a friend.'

Oakley subsided. Turning to Harris, he said wearily, 'All right, Sergeant. Get the demo over, but quickly.'

Chapter 43

From his hiding place alongside the school, Denny Rees watched the school march out. Then he watched the van arrive, saw Carver talking to Hart, and finally the arrival of the television cameramen.

Then he saw Carver walk along the line of lads with posters and speak to each one. As Carver reached the last, Denny moved. This was his signal. He picked up the box Carver had given him. It was small, but heavy. From one end the red top of a toggle on a cord stuck out. He knew what he had to do. Slip it into the broom cupboard, pull the toggle, close the door, and then leave by the window.

He'd gone over it one break time. He was very handy with windows, was Denny. He could do it all in five minutes and Carver said he had twenty. When he'd done the job, he was to get over the fence at the back of the school and vanish. As far as the school was concerned he was sick. He'd been off for two days and his mum had sent his sister in with a note. She didn't care much what he did as long as he kept out of her way.

He crept along the concrete to the wall below the window. It was open. He'd fixed that early this morning – and the cupboard door too. If someone had shut the cupboard again he'd have to open it. He could do that in three minutes. That made eight in all. He'd worked everything out. He was handy at things like that, was Denny. And when he'd done this job, he was in with Carver, and that left Stebson with the boys.

He eased back the window catch and gently lifted up the box and rested it on the sill inside. With a careful last look round -- always double check – he heaved himself up nimbly and was over the sill and into the passage. No sweat.

Once again he looked round. The corridor was empty. He could see right to the other end. The glass doors were clear.

He tiptoed along and in half a minute, no more. no less, he was by the broom cupboard. Carefully he set down the box. He could feel his heart going faster now and the shirt on his back was wet with perspiration.

The door was locked. Some joker had locked it. He bit his lip and felt in his pocket for the plastic card he used. Not there. He felt in his other pocket. There it was. He breathed again.

He placed his hand on the door by the lock and slowly brought up the card in the other.

'You're nicked, Rees.'

He leapt round and tried to run from the voice. But he ran full tilt into what seemed to be an enormous chest. Somebody held him very firmly.

'Got him, Alan?'

'Too right, Tucker.'

'Now, listen, Denny boy,' said Tucker. 'If you don't want us to put you in that cupboard with that little box and lock the door, you'd better do some very quick talking.'

123

Chapter 44

The first cameraman sauntered up to Hart.

'O.K., squire. What have you brought us round here for? You said something special. That usually means something special, not a bunch of ageing skinheads with a pathetic attempt to break the Race Relations Act – and not even spelt right at that.'

Hart smiled uneasily.

'All I know is that something big's coming off here. I let you know. You're here. From now on it's your job.'

'And what are you doing, then?'

'I'm hanging about in case anything happens. Then I may do lineage for the nationals.'

'And that's all you're saying, eh?'

'What else do you want? There isn't anything else.'

'I can see that myself, squire. We've come down here, we miss the chance of a bit of footage at the main road there – traffic snarl-up and so on – to stick around in a cul-de-sac looking at an empty school and six rejects from the system! I should have my head tested.'

He signalled to his colleagues. 'Let's get it back in the car, we might just catch that demo at the High Road.'

'Wait a minute,' called Hart. He held up his hand.

From one of the streets nearby came the sound of police sirens. The cameramen halted, turned about and lifted their gear into position again.

'What's up with chummy, eh?'

Benson and the other sandwich men had broken ranks and gathered round Carver, who was trying vainly to get them back into place.

'Listen, don't panic. Only another couple of minutes.'

'That's the Old Bill, mate. I'm leaving.'

'You're not, you know. It's not us, it's some other place.'

'It's coming closer, Eddie.'

'No you bloody don't.' Carver grabbed one lad by the shirt front and thrust him against the gate.

'That's a bit more like it,' said the first cameraman and began filming. 'We'll find out what it's about in a minute. Let's hope it makes sense.'

'Now,' said Carver.

'Now what?'

Nothing happened. Closer came the police siren, and in the further distance sounded the brass of the school band and the song:

'Grange Hill, Grange Hill,
They're taking you away.'

Carver quelled his little trouble and lined up his men again.

'Ho hum,' said the cameraman. 'What now?'

'Tell you what,' said his colleague, 'we hang on here and catch the demo coming back to the school.'

'Don't get me over-excited, lad,' came the reply.

'Hey, look! Over there by the school.'

All turned as if on swivels. The main door of the school opened and across the yard strolled three girls – Trisha Yates, Pamela Cartwright and Susi MacMahon. Carver's men stared as the three drew nearer. At about ten paces they halted. The two groups looked at one another in silence for a second, then Trisha Yates spoke.

'You think that's smart, Carver – these posters?'

Carver looked her over insolently and seemed about to reply when she went on: 'Well, how do you like these posters, then?'

From behind their backs the girls produced sheets of card lettered in red paint. The message was brief and clear:

'HEAR THAT WHISTLE BLOW.'

'TAKE OFF, CARVER.'

'YOU HAVE BEEN RUMBLED.'

Carver's poster parade began to break up as the TV men began to film. Carver moved forward as if to leap over the school fence, when Trisha called:

'I wouldn't if I were you.'

'Look at that,' yelled Booga Benson.

All stood as if nailed to the spot. Out from the school main door, a small procession made its way. First came Tucker and Alan, and behind them Mr Thomson the caretaker.

And right in the middle, white faced and scared, marched Denny Rees.

As they came closer, Alan held aloft a small box.

Carver stared. For an instant he seemed unable to speak or move.

At that moment, round one corner at the head of the road careered a police car, siren sounding. And around the other marched the head of the school parade.

'. . . What more can I say?

Councilman, Mr Councilman,

Give Grange Hill a Chance,

A little chance,

Give Grange Hill a chance.'

'Well, well,' said the first TV man, swinging up his camera. 'Thank you, brother. We're spoilt for choice.'

In the side road the engine of the grey van came to life and the Carver sandwich men bolted in all directions.

Booga Benson, his reflexes working to the last, launched himself at the cameraman and thousands of pounds' worth of equipment were scattered over the pavement with a crunching sound.

Hart rushed forward.

'Is it in the can?' he called anxiously.

'Yes, squire, it is,' came the reply, 'and you're carrying it.'